EVERYTHING FOR LOVE

EVERYTHING FOR LOVE
A BEAUMONT SERIES / BEAUMONT SERIES NEXT
GENERATION NOVELLA
HEIDI MCLAUGHLIN

© 2023

COVER DESIGN: OkayCreations.
EDITING: Edits by Amy
COPY EDITING: YR Editor

 Created with Vellum

NEWEST RELEASES

Before I'm Gone

Sangria

Stranded With the One

THE SEAPORT SERIES

The Lobster Trap

The Love in Sunsets

THE BEAUMONT SERIES READING ORDER

Prequels:

Forever Mason

Finding My Way

~

Forever My Girl

My Everything

My Unexpected Forever

Finding My Forever

12 Days of Forever

My Kind of Forever

Forever Our Boys

Holding Onto Forever

My Unexpected Love

Chasing My Forever

Peyton & Noah

Fighting For Our Forever

A Beaumont Family Christmas

Fourth Down

Give Me Forever

Everything For Love

This sleeping on the couch shit is for the birds. My back aches. I sit up and place my bare feet on the cold floor. A shiver runs through me, causing another ache and I cringe as my back tightens. Yet here I am night after night.

I head into the bathroom, which is down the hall from what used to be my bedroom, to shower and get ready for work. Yesterday when I checked my appointments, they were staggered. Nothing back-to-back or overlapping. I really hate it when appointments overlap. It never fails, the new mom will come in with a million and one questions about her child because she saw something on TV, or her friend read about some rare disease, and she's certain her child has it now.

When I get out of the shower Aubrey's in the kitchen talking on the phone. She quiets when she hears me and probably waits until I close the bedroom door before she starts up again. I have no idea who she talks to this early in the morning but if I had to guess it's likely her mother. After

I dress, I go wake Mack and Amelie for school and then take my chance in the kitchen.

"Morning."

She says nothing.

Sighing heavily, I open the refrigerator and grab what I need to make breakfast. "Do you want breakfast?"

"No."

At least she answered me. I know I'm putting off the inevitable, asking her what's wrong, but it's because I don't want to hear how I've failed as a husband. Everything I do is wrong. I didn't buy the right bread. I didn't park the car straight. She was late to yoga because I didn't come home five minutes earlier. The list of trivial shit goes on and on.

When the kids come into the kitchen, Aubrey brightens and pastes on a happy face. Or maybe she's truly happy to see them and just hates me. Mack and Amelie sit at the table and wait for breakfast. Mack's texting one of his friends and Amelie's tattling.

"That's enough," I say, only for Aubrey to shoot daggers at me.

"Don't talk to her like that."

"She doesn't need to tattle on Mack for having his phone out at the table. There isn't any goddamn food there yet."

That's one of Aubrey's rules, no phones at the table. Which means I have to keep my phone in the other room with the ringer on when I'm on call because, you know, ignoring patients goes against a doctor's oath and all that.

Mack comes around the island and helps plate their food. He takes the two plates to the table and sets one down in front of Amelie. I use the quick break to look at my schedule to verify what I already know. No patients until ten. I shoot a text off to my staff and tell them I'll be in later

2

this morning. The kids eat in silence while I stand on the other side of Aubrey, waiting for her to say something.

Minutes later, Mack says, "Mrs. Westbury is outside. Bye." He rushes to the door while Amelie gives Aubrey and me a hug goodbye.

"Have a good day."

"Aren't you leaving?" she asks.

I shake my head slowly. "Nope. We're going to talk."

"I have nothing to say, Nick."

"Bullshit. You have plenty to say but you keep shit bottled up. Let's have it, Aubrey. What did I do this time?"

She scoffs. "At least you know you're guilty."

"Of what?" I throw my hands up. "What did I do? Or didn't do?"

"Nothing. You're perfect." The sarcasm coming from her is deadly.

I shake my head. "We both know that's not true. I can't force it out of you, but we can't keep living like this. We need to talk about what's going on."

Her eyes are life fire as she stares at me. "Fine. You want to know?"

"I do. Lay it on me." For emphasis and because I can be an asshole, I spread my arms out wide.

"I know you're having an affair with Brianna and Josie."

Okay, I wasn't expecting that. My arms fall. Brianna is one of my new nurses, not two years out of school. She's definitely pretty, but in a long-term relationship with someone she went to college with. Earlier I was in love with Josie and now I'm having an affair with her. I can't fucking win.

Regardless, having an office affair isn't something I'd ever do. I pride myself on having morals and integrity.

"What?"

"You heard me," she says. "The late night calls. The *not* coming home after work. I followed her once."

"Why would you do that?"

"To catch you in the act."

I scrub my hand over my face. "Aubrey, I'm not having an affair with Brianna or anyone else. I have never been unfaithful to you."

Another scoff. "You're in love with Josie Westbury."

"Good God. I am not. I was over her when I met you."

"I'll never believe you. I see the way you look at her."

"No, you see what you want to see. We're cordial because of Noah and Mack. Nothing more."

"Don't you think it's funny that Mack's so close to Noah, but Noah's not close to Amelie?"

"Up until recently, you were close with Noah. And Paige. Hell, the entire family and now the bond Mack and Noah have is an issue?"

Aubrey says nothing.

I pinch the bridge of my nose and sigh. "Noah and Mack have a lot in common, Aubrey. You know this. That's it. There's nothing going on. I'm not having an affair with anyone. Is that what this is about?"

"Is what about?"

I know Aubrey isn't stupid, but she's acting like she is. "Seriously? You don't talk to me for months. You barely look at me. We haven't—"

"Don't you dare talk about sex with me, Nick. You don't even sleep in the same room as me."

"And why is that, Aubrey?"

I wait.

"Because you've rebuffed me for over a year. There comes a point when a man's pride is hurt. No matter what I did, you pushed me away." I groan and pace the kitchen.

4

I love this woman but damn it if she doesn't drive me batty.

"I think we should move."

"What?"

Aubrey nods. "I think we should move."

"Did you find a house you want to buy or something?"

She shakes her head. "No, Doctors Without Borders needs help. I mean, they always need help. I want to move back to South Africa."

"No," I blurt out right away. It's no different than when Josie and I had the same conversation all those years ago and she said the same thing.

"Excuse me? You can't tell me no."

"You're right. I can't because you're free to do whatever the hell you want, as long as it doesn't mess up this family. There's no way in hell we're moving out of Beaumont. Mack's in high school. He has a lot going for him right now. Why would you want to mess that up for him?"

"What about me?" she screams. "What about what I want?"

"What the hell do you want, Aubrey? Tell me. Do you want your husband?"

"No," she says quietly.

It takes me a minute, but the words sink in.

"You don't want me?"

My wife shakes her head slowly. "I hate it here. I'm bored. This small-town life, it might be good for you, being the town doctor that all the women fawn over, but I hate it. I never agreed to live here."

"You did, when we got married," I point out. "You encouraged me to return here and maintain a relationship with Noah."

"Well, I was wrong. And I'm done."

"You're done? What does that even mean?"

Aubrey can't look me in the eyes. I bend and lean forward, giving her no choice. I reach out to touch her and she moves away.

"Really, Aubrey?"

"I don't know what you want from me."

"I've said the same thing to you," I point out. "Apparently, the life you've lived for the last eighteen years isn't what you've wanted this entire time. And yet, after two kids, you've failed to mention this. Today alone, you've accused me of having an affair with one of my nurses and being in love with Josie, who I'd like to point out is your friend."

"She's only my friend because of you."

"Okay? That doesn't make her less of a friend, Aubrey. Do you mean to tell me all those shopping trips you've gone on with her, you did so to appease me? Because I never asked you to be friends with Josie. Or anyone else in town. I never asked you to join the PTA, to volunteer us to run the school carnival, girl scout troop, and whatever else the kids have done over the years. You did that and it certainly wasn't to appease me."

I pull out one of the dining room chairs, hoping she'll do the same. When she doesn't, I ask, "Can we please sit and talk?"

She shakes her head, but eventually sits down. Instantly, she covers her face. I'd like to think she's crying, but she's not.

"Aside from moving to South Africa, what can I do to get you through this funk?"

"Nothing," she says automatically.

"Not a thing, huh? Just going to destroy our family?"

"I'm not happy, Nick."

"All right, so let me fix it. Let's find a happy medium that gets us through the next couple of years. We'll go when Mack graduates."

"That's too long."

"It's two years, Aubrey. We're not taking him out of school and ruining his chances at getting a scholarship."

"He doesn't need to play sports, Nick. There are so many other life lessons to learn out there. Not everything revolves around football and baseball."

"When you're his age, it does."

"If you love me, you'll do this."

I shake my head as anger boils. "Don't do that, Aubrey. That's unfair."

"It's what I want."

"Two years," I tell her. "Give us two more years and we'll go. I'll sell the practice, the house, and we'll take Amelie and go."

Aubrey sits for a moment, staring at everything but me. She won't make eye contact and it bothers me. There's something else going on in her head and she's not letting me in. Not that I blame her. This is the most we've talked in months.

Again, I reach for her hand, but she draws it back. "We're not magically fixed because we're talking."

"No, of course not."

"And I'm not convinced you're not cheating on me."

I groan. "I'm not having an affair."

"Then where are you getting sex from? Because it's not from me."

I hold up my hand, mostly to piss her off. "Where are *you* getting sex from?" Her mouth drops open and then closes. "Is that what's going on here? You don't want me, so who do you want?"

7

"No one."

It's my turn to scoff and I do so loudly. "Now who's not being honest, Aubrey?"

She says nothing.

"What's his name? Does he come here after I leave for work? Is that why you asked me why I wasn't leaving this morning?"

She still says nothing, but I can see the guilt—or something—all over her face.

"What's his fucking name, Aubrey?"

Without thinking, I push away from the table and the bowl of fruit goes flying, crashing onto the floor. Glass shatters and spreads across the hardwood.

"Look at what you did."

"It was an accident." I head toward the closet to get the broom. When I come back, she's sobbing. I say nothing to her as I clean up the mess and ignore the crocodile tears. "I'm going to ask you again, Aubrey. What do you want?"

Another sob.

"Are you crying because I broke the bowl or because you're projecting your guilt onto me with this affair bullshit. I mean, I guess it makes sense. Up until the day you began turning away from my advances, we fucked like rabbits. Then boom, you have a headache. Do you still have a headache, or do you want to go fuck?" It's crass. I know this, but anger does funny things to one's thought process.

"You're being a pig."

"Yep." I agree with her. "What do you want, Aubrey?"

"A divorce."

Even as she says the word, I don't want to believe her. But there it is. It's the freedom she wants. I dump the glass and fruit into the garbage and walk down the hall to the closet. After putting the broom and dustpan away, I slam the door. Not once. Not twice. But three times. "Fuck!" I yell as I run my hands roughly through my hair, tugging at the ends. Going back into the kitchen, she still sits there, staring at who knows what.

"Is that what you want, Aubrey? Do you really want a divorce?"

She nods.

I nod as well but she's not looking at me. "You can have it, but you're not taking the kids. I won't allow it."

"I'm their mother," she roars and spins in the chair to face me.

"And I'm their father," I say, pointing at my chest. "You're not uprooting them to go back to a country they've never been to before so they can live in a yurt while you play nurse. Which, I'll point out, you haven't done in over ten years. You don't even have a valid nursing license!" I scream the last bit as I head towards the front door.

"It's in the works and will be valid by the time I get there."

"You can have the divorce, but you're not taking the kids. Merry fucking Christmas." Those are the words I say as I head out the front door.

2

We had weeks of peace and then all hell breaks loose. Apparently, I wasn't moving fast enough for her—with what, I'm unsure—but dragging my feet didn't sit well with her.

Like any other night, I come home and find the kids sitting at the table doing their homework. After a quick hi, I take my bag into my office and think about sitting down to relax for a bit after dealing with multiple cases of the flu, a bout of chickenpox, and a baby who won't stop crying every time his mother picks him up. After an exam, I noticed some bruising she couldn't explain, and I had no choice but to follow my gut instinct and call child services. By the time they arrived, she had broken down and admitted to hitting him. Fun fucking times.

"Come in," I say after a knock sounds.

"Hey," Mack says as he comes into the room. "Um, Betty Paige invited me to go skiing in Vermont after Christmas. Do you think I can go? Noah's going to be there, and I think it'll be fun."

"Did you talk to your mom?"

Mack's face drops and I do everything I can to not roll my eyes.

"I'll take care of it. I don't mind as long as it's cool with Liam and Josie. I'll call them later."

"Thanks, Dad."

Mack leaves and I wait for the door to close before I let out a groan as I grip the side of my desk. I honestly don't know what to do. Not with Aubrey, the kids, or my marriage. Obviously, the answer is to get a divorce, but that's Aubrey's solution. Not mine.

Knowing Aubrey's in the bedroom, I head into the kitchen and start dinner. I suppose when she stopped doing things like making the kids' food, it should've been a sign something was up with her. But nope, I covered for her because I love her and I'm her husband. That's what husbands should do.

"Amelie, set the table please," I say as I fill a pot with water and set it on the stove. The pantry is stocked but unorganized, another pet peeve. I can't help that I like things neat and orderly. It's in my nature as a doctor. With a box of noodles and a jar of pasta sauce in my hands, I'm back at the stove.

"I don't want to," Amelie says.

"I didn't ask you what you wanted. I told you to set the table."

"No, why can't Mack do it?"

This mini-Aubrey version is going to send me to an early grave. The pre-teen hormones are no joke and if there was medication for it, I'd have that child on them so damn fast.

"Because I told you to do it. I don't want to say it again, Amelie. Set the table."

"Oh my God, you're so mean. Everything is so unfair. Mack never has to do anything."

Mack opens his mouth, but I send him a warning glare. The last thing I want is for this battle to continue. In five minutes, she'll be over it and things will calm down until the next fight starts.

I pull some ground chicken from the refrigerator and toss it into a frying pan and end up finding a box of Texas toast in the freezer. It's not much of a dinner, especially with Mack growing like a weed, but it's something.

Twenty minutes later, Aubrey emerges from the bedroom and sits down. I want to ask why she's even bothering, but I bite my tongue. I don't want to fight in front of the kids. Our issues are ours. Not theirs.

However, halfway through dinner, everything changes. Aubrey sits up and gets the kids' attention. She has mine, too, because suddenly, I'm on edge.

"Your dad and I wanted to talk to you tonight."

Right off, I know this isn't going to be good. We haven't discussed anything about the kids, other than I'm not allowing them to go with her. "Aubrey—" I warn. She doesn't look at me, but back and forth between our children. My stomach rolls. "Don't do what I think you're about to do."

"It needs to be done, Nick."

"No, it doesn't. Not now." Not days before fucking Christmas.

"Your dad and I have decided to get a divorce."

Silence.

And confusion.

Mack looks from his mom to me. "What?"

"Sorry, bud," I tell him as I reach for his hand. "This

isn't how I wanted you and your sister to find out and it's definitely not the right time."

Amelie starts sobbing and goes to her mom for a hug. I sigh heavily, wishing none of this was happening.

"It'll be okay," Aubrey says to Amelie and then reaches for Mack's hand. "You guys are going to love Johannesburg."

As if in slow motion, realization washes over Mack. He takes his hand away from his mother's grip and stands. "I'm not moving," he says. "You can't make me."

"I can," Aubrey says. "I'm your mother."

"You don't have to move," I tell him. "Aubrey, can you please stop? None of this is what we talked about, and I already told you, you can go. I'll give you the divorce, but you're not taking the kids. God, why couldn't you have waited until we had a discussion on how to tell them because this is not it."

"Because I want out!" she yells.

"Then leave." I point to the door. "No one is keeping you here. I can take care of them. I do it every morning while you stand around acting like someone has hurt *you* when all you're doing is hurting our family. If you want to go, then go."

"I'll go with you, Mommy," Amelie says, almost pleading with her mother.

"Go to your rooms. Both of you," I tell them.

Mack starts toward his room, but Amelie just stares at me. I'm on the verge of losing it. All of it, and I know it won't be pretty. Aubrey sits there, with her arm wrapped around our daughter, as if they're protecting each other. I pinch the bridge of my nose and take a deep breath.

"Amelie, I'm not going to tell you again."

"You didn't ask her," Aubrey says.

"I'm not asking her, Aubrey. I'm her father and I told her to go to her bedroom." I start to stand, ready and willing to go to battle with either of them, when Mack comes back into the room.

"Come on, Amelie. Let's go watch a movie." We make eye contact, and that's when I see he's fighting back tears.

Fuck this.

As soon as I hear his door shut, I move next to Aubrey and keep my voice as low as possible. "What in the hell was that? Seriously, Aubrey. You're a nurse. You know better than to put children in the middle of this type of shit."

"You're scaring me," she says.

I nod and move a seat away from her. "Is this better, or would you like me to go into my office and call you to discuss the bomb you just dropped on our kids?"

"It was time."

"Don't you think we should've discussed how we were going to approach this, and when? Do you think it's fair to ruin their Christmas? They're children, Aubrey. Still forming their frontal lobes, and this is a memory you want to tie into on their favorite holiday? They're never going to forget this. Ever. It's going to be ingrained."

"Fine. All right. But it's done, and they know they're moving."

I scrub my hand over my face and groan. "They're not moving. You're not taking them."

"I am."

"Then I'll file kidnapping charges. Is that what you want? Do you want the feds to stop you at the airport and make a scene? Why are you doing this?"

"Because they're my babies."

"They are, and they're mine, too. And you're not

thinking about what's best for them right now. You're thinking about you and how you're going to hurt me."

"You've hurt me."

"How? Tell me how and I'll get down on my knees and beg for your forgiveness. Tell me how I've hurt you, Aubrey."

"The affair," she says quietly.

This time, I roll my eyes. "I'm not having an affair." I pull my phone out of my pocket, unlock the screen, which is her birthday, and hand it to her. "Go through it."

"I'm sure you deleted everything."

"Right."

I leave my phone there and go to the refrigerator to get a beer. Across the room of our open concept house, our Christmas tree sits in the front window. Two weeks ago, the kids and I decorated it while Aubrey stayed in the bedroom with a headache. Maybe that should've been my wake-up call.

"I booked flights to Johannesburg," she says.

"When?"

"The day after they get out of school." Aubrey stands and comes toward me.

I shake my head slowly. "No, and I'm done having this conversation with you. Tomorrow, you'll hear from my lawyer."

I put my unopened beer back in the refrigerator and head down the hall to Mack's room. Knocking first, I open the door slowly to find him sitting on the edge of his bed, talking on the phone, with Amelie asleep.

Mack stands. "I don't want to move," he says quietly so as not to wake his sister. "Please don't do this to me."

"You're not moving. Who's on the phone?"

"Paige."

16

"Hang up and come see me in my office." I shut his door and head to my office. It's my space and the only place I'll get peace right now. Seconds later, Mack's sitting on my couch, which is also currently my bed. At least I have the keen sense of mind to fold my blankets in the morning so the space is somewhat presentable.

"I'm sorry for what your mom did at dinner. This is not how I wanted you and your sister to find out."

"What's going on?"

"I'm going to be honest with you. Your mom wants to move back to South Africa. Apparently, she's wanted this for a while, but felt like she couldn't say anything. I don't think it's right that she takes you and Amelie. In fact, I'm dead set against it."

"I don't want to go, Dad. Amelie does, though."

I nod. "I figured. Honestly, I'm not surprised. She's young enough to still adjust and forge a new path, but you . . ." I put my hand on his leg. "You have a lot going for you right now."

"Please don't make me go."

"I'm going to do my best, Mack. I have to talk to a lawyer tomorrow and figure some things out."

"Are you going to move out?"

"Definitely not. Your mom and I have coexisted for a while now. I'll just have to watch where I step."

Mack's eyes rim with tears. "I hate her. She's trying to ruin my life."

"Hate's a strong word, bud. Right now, your mom's angry with me, and she knows this is how to hurt me, through you and your sister."

"But why does she want to hurt me?"

"My guess is she doesn't see it as hurting you but protecting you from me."

17

Mack's tears fall down his cheeks. I pull him into my arms and let him cry. I never wanted this for my children and never thought in a million years Aubrey would want it either. Both our parents are still married and going strong. This news is going to devastate them. Although, I imagine her parents are happy she's coming back to them.

"Promise me something, Mack."

"What?" he asks in a broken voice.

"If you can't talk to me about something in your life, like how you're dealing with the divorce, talk to Noah. Okay?"

Mack nods and wipes his tears. "Okay."

3

The last time I sat in the chair at my lawyer's office, it was for advice on how I'd adopt Noah. Liam had just returned, and my life circled the drain. Everything I thought I knew, thought I had, disappeared in the blink of an eye. Or the roar of a motorcycle engine in this case. The moment he came back to Beaumont, I knew there was no way Josie and I were going to last. She could have denied it all she wanted, but I knew the truth. She was, and always had been, head over heels in love with him. I was stupid enough to think I'd be enough for her to get over him. At the time, I probably was.

My lawyer comes into his office, clears his throat, and then sits down. He has a manila folder with him. It's thin and lacking contents but I see my name on the front and imagine it's on the tab as well. What a shitty client I am, never giving him any business. Not even malpractice. Maybe that makes me a saint. Who knows.

I'm uncomfortable. The office has a smell to it. I can't pinpoint what it is, other than an old, musty odor. Everything in here is brown. Brown desk, chairs, drapes, bookcases, and carpet, to go with spots of red, blue, and green from various law books. And the manila folder. It's drab, lifeless, and it makes me think being a lawyer is a boring job.

Lesley Wroughton clears his throat again and clasps his hands on his desk. "My secretary said this was urgent."

"It is," I say and then wonder if all his clients say the same thing. No one likes to wait. "My wife wants a divorce. I don't, but that's not the problem."

"What is then?"

"She wants to take my kids to South Africa to live with her and I'm not okay with that."

"I see."

Does he? What exactly does he see?

He opens the manila folder and makes some inaudible sound, almost like a huff and a tsk combined. "If I'm doing my math correctly, you have one child and he's well above the age of eighteen."

Oh good lord.

"I believe you're looking at the case I came to you last time for. Since then, I've married and have two children, Mack and Amelie. They're sixteen and ten, respectively."

"I see." He jots some notes down. "And your wife's name isn't Josie?"

"No, it's Aubrey."

"Okay. How long have you been married?"

I fill him in on everything, from where we met, to our wedding, the birth of Mack, and then Amelie. I tell him I'm the primary breadwinner and that Aubrey and I agreed she didn't need to work while raising the kids. She maintained an office in my practice and would fill in when one of the nurses was out, but mainly focused on research and women's health. I made it known around town that if a woman couldn't afford care, they could come see Aubrey and not worry about paying. It was shortly after Peyton and Noah got married, Aubrey decided to stop coming in. Eventually, the office space turned into storage, and she has since let her nursing license lapse.

"All right. And now she wants to take the kids on vacation?"

"No, to live," I remind him. "It's where her parents live."

His hand scribbles over his notepad, pauses, and then writes again. "Will Mrs. Ashford have a lawyer in the divorce proceedings?"

"I don't know the answer to that. What I do know is she's purchased one-way airline tickets for the day after school finishes for the holidays and plans to take the kids with her. Mack refuses to go but Amelie wants to go. I don't want them to go at all."

This entire time, I'm talking to his head. He never looks up. He stares at the legal pad that he's scribbling on and fires off questions.

"Okay, we can file a temporary order barring Mrs. Ashford from taking the children out of the country. But I'll be honest, it's paperwork and you'll have to report them as kidnapped in order for the authorities to do anything."

"What about their passports?"

"Are they US citizens?"

"Dual," I tell him. "Aubrey was born in Cape Town."

He finally looks at me and nods. "As their mother, she can get their passports reissued without your permission. The injunction will keep them stateside, if you happen to be there when she leaves with them."

"So, I'll have to watch her?"

He nods. "I'll have to look up the law and see what kind of agreement we have, but child custody is hard when other countries are involved. If she's a citizen and goes to the government with a story against you, they're liable to protect her and the children. It's all very messy. Can I ask whether you hit her? Or the kids?"

"No, absolutely not."

"Are you a drinker? Smoker? Drug user?"

"Social drinker, but that's it."

"Is there anything Mrs. Ashford can use against you?"

"Not if she's telling the truth, but I'll be honest, we haven't been on great terms for about a year, the past few months have been worse. I'm not sure I trust her to be honest about much."

"What happened a year ago?"

I shake my head slowly. "I have no idea. It was like a switch flipped and she was no longer interested in me. I tried, but after a while a man gives up."

"And seeks attention elsewhere?"

"No, I've been faithful to Aubrey through all of this. I have never strayed, despite her accusing me of doing so."

"You said your daughter wants to go with your wife?"

I nod. "From my experience, it's the mother-daughter bond. Amelie's young, impressionable, and extremely close to her mom. Aubrey coddles her and gives her what she wants. Amelie uses that and plays me against her mom all the time. She's also a pre-teen and those years suck."

Lesley laughs. "Believe me, I know." He scribbles some more. "Has there been any discussion of a custody arrangement?"

"No," I tell him. "She's adamant that she's taking the children because she's their mother."

"She can say what she wants, but the law is on your side."

Thank God.

"With that said, I like to encourage my clients to figure out a solution before they file. The courts appreciate it, and it makes it a lot easier on the kids. Do you think you and Mrs. Ashford can come to an agreement beforehand?"

"I'm not sure. We want two different things. Our son excels in school here. I don't want to take him out of school to move across the world. He'd have to give up what he loves, football and baseball, not to mention his friends and classmates. I proposed we move as a family after Mack graduates from high school in two years. I thought she'd go for that, but she refuses, she wants to go now and then asked for a divorce."

Lesley sighs. "I rarely suggest this, but have you considered staying here and letting your wife take your daughter with her?"

"What?" Surely, I've misheard him.

"Here me out," he says. "From what you're telling me, Mrs. Ashford is determined to return to her home country with her children. Well, one child. Mack is old enough to decide where he wants to live, and a judge wouldn't force him to leave the country if he didn't want to. With him out of the equation, that leaves your youngest. She's close to her mother?"

"Extremely."

"And Mrs. Ashford is demanding to take the children, regardless?"

I nod.

"As your lawyer, I'm going to suggest you let her."

"Excuse me?"

Wroughton holds his hand up. "If she takes your daughter without your permission, you'll report her for kidnapping. The police will arrest your wife in front of your daughter. Do you want that?"

I shake my head slowly.

"If she takes your daughter and you report her for kidnapping, you're then fighting a foreign country to get your daughter back, which honestly could be extremely challenging and costly. Playing nice is a much better option, and tucking your pride is much easier than pitting your daughter against you because you had her mother arrested."

My hands grip the arm rests. I can't believe what he's telling me to do—let Aubrey take Amelie to Johannesburg—and then what?

"What if I never see her again?"

He looks through his notes. "You've been there before?"

I nod. "Yes, with Doctors Without Borders."

"I'm assuming your passport is in good standing?"

"Yes."

He shrugs as if the answer is obvious. "Go visit. Hell, volunteer for a month. Do it every few months, but go there, be present. And if the time comes when you need the courts help to get your daughter back, it'll be proven that you were there for her."

I don't want to admit it, but what he says makes sense, even if I hate every part of it. I don't know if I can give up Amelie. We may butt heads right now, but she's still my daughter. My baby. I can't imagine her living across the world, living the lifestyle her mother wants to live. I doubt Amelie would survive.

"Do you really think that's best?"

"I've told you what the alternative is, unless you can get Mrs. Ashford to stay here."

That's unlikely.

"I guess I have a lot to think about where Amelie's concerned. About the divorce, though, I'd like to move forward."

He nods and starts writing again.

After the appointment, I go home, hoping Aubrey's there and wishing she isn't. What a fucking feeling to have.

Inside, soft music plays from the bedroom. I make my way down the hall and stand in the doorway. Aubrey's dancing, swaying to the music. We used to do this at night, after the kids went to bed. It was our thing. Our way to calm down before turning in for the night. Watching her I try to remember when we stopped dancing, when we stopped caring about each other. The thing is, I still care about her. Hell, I love her. Am still in love with her.

She turns and startles. The happy expression she had morphs into anger. Hatred. When and why did this happen to us?

"Don't be mad," I say to her. "I came home to talk. I don't want to fight with you, Aubrey."

"Then give me what I want."

"It's not that easy. You want to destroy our family and take my children away from me. Just thinking of not having them here, in the house they grew up in, rips my heart out. They're my life. You're my life. There isn't anything I wouldn't do for the three of you . . . except this. I can't. We can't do this to our son."

"I don't want to be here anymore, Nick."

"I know, so let's compromise."

"What do you have in mind?"

I take a big breath and lean harder into the doorjamb. "Liam and Josie have invited Mack to go skiing in Vermont after Christmas. Their entire family is going. Noah, too. I told Mack he can go." I hold up my hand when she starts to say something. "Yes, I should've talked to you, but I'll be honest, Aubs, you haven't been the easiest to talk to as of late."

"Go on."

"With Mack with the Westburys', why don't I fly with you and Amelie to Johannesburg. I'll help you get settled. I'm worried about Amelie and how she'll acclimate. I gather you're heading to a village?"

She nods.

"Have you thought about schooling? Living arrangements? Her activities? You're selling her on this lifestyle, and I'm afraid she doesn't understand it."

"I'll figure it out when I get there."

"Aubrey, what are you going to do with a ten-year-old who is used to living like this?" I wave my hands in a grandiose gesture to everything she and the kids have. Everything I've provided for them, to give them a comfortable life.

"She's going to learn material things aren't needed in the real world."

I nod and want to wish her luck, but I don't say anything. There's no way I can let Amelie go to South Africa with her mom. It would be like her going alone.

"So, that's my offer. We can leave after Christmas."

"No," she says pointedly. "I plan to spend Christmas with my parents."

"They don't celebrate Christmas," I remind her.

She has nothing to say.

"Do you really want to interrupt their Christmas?"

"It's too late," she tells me. "I have to be there by the twenty-first. I've already talked to Amelie, she wants to go with me, Nick."

"I know she does. I'm only trying to protect her from disappointment."

"What if she loves it there?"

I fight back a wave of emotions. "I did, when I went, but

28

I was there with a different purpose. I fell in love there. It'll always hold a special place in my heart, and I hope for your sake, Amelie feels the same way."

"She will."

I inhale deeply, wishing things were different. "So, it's settled?"

"What about Mack?"

Shrugging, I shake my head. "I'll be back before school starts. It'll all work out."

She stares at me, and I wonder what's going on in her mind. I wish like hell she would open up to me, tell where all of this anger, resentment, and hatred is coming from. The sudden dislike for Josie is concerning. I'm tempted to ask Josie if something happened, but it's not my place because I'm trying to respect Aubrey's friendship. I fear asking would somehow get back to my wife and I would pay dearly.

Aubrey tilts her head. Is she trying to see through me?

"Thanks."

Thanks? That's all I get?

"Yep." I don't tell her she's welcome, because she's not. I hate that this is what our lives have come to. I push away from the door, needing space.

"Hey, Nick?" She calls after me. Reluctantly, I turn back toward the room. "Despite me asking for a divorce, I still love you. I just . . . I need to get out of here. I feel like I'm suffocating."

I say nothing.

4

$\mathcal{S}$he's suffocating. What am I even supposed to say to her? How does one respond? I feel like my life has been a lie, at least the part with her. Here I am, thinking we have the perfect life with two perfect kids, and my perfect wife is suffocating, but never says anything. When we made love, was she suffocating then? How am I supposed to unpack any of this without losing my mind?

After the kids get home and we have dinner, I go out. I need to be alone. I need space to think and process my failed marriage. I had hoped that with me suggesting I go with her, she'd change her mind about taking Amelie, and give up on the notion that our daughter needs this life experience. I know Amelie probably better than she knows herself. She's not going to be happy once the newness of the adventure wears off. She doesn't like dirt or being overly hot. Sharing isn't her idea of fun either and I'm fairly certain Aubrey hasn't told her that she doesn't get to bring any of her electronic devices or any of her things when they go out on a mission. Which, knowing the agency, will be right away. Then what's Aubrey going to do with a bored ten-year-old who isn't accustomed to the lifestyle Aubrey grew up with? Should we have introduced the kids to the work their grandparents do? Absolutely. Did we? No, we failed in that department of parenting.

I drive around for hours until I find myself in the parking lot of the liquor store. The red sign hums from the electricity surging through the neon bulbs. The Q is out and has been for at least ten, if not fifteen years. My phone rings and Josie's name shows on the screen in my car. I press the button.

"Hey."

"Hi, just checking to make sure Mack is still coming with us?"

"Yeah, he is."

"Great. I'll let Noah and Paige know. Just pack him whatever warm clothes he has. I'll order him a ski suit thingy or whatever they're called."

"Thanks. I can pay you."

"Nah, don't worry about it."

"Does he need to bring anything?"

"No, I think between Jenna, Katelyn, and myself we'll have it all covered."

I nod and look out the window. "Thanks, Josie. You don't know how much this means to him. And to me."

"It's our pleasure."

We hang up and I sit there, contemplating if I want to go into the store or just go home. I hate that I left Mack there without a buffer. He doesn't deserve what's going on. Neither does Amelie. Siblings pitted against each other because parents can't figure their shit out can't be fun. He wants to stay. She wants to go. The Ashford men want one thing, while the women in our lives want something that tears our family apart.

It's now or never. I go inside and grab a six pack of bottles. Always bottles. And I pay in cash because that's the only thing they take. I suppose that's why the Q is still out on the sign. The books are cooked. Mind you, this is also the place in town that never looks twice at an ID, so I guess it's no surprise. It doesn't matter if the name on it says Santa Claus, they'll let you buy beer. None of the cops in town have ever busted them because they'd all have to admit they bought beer illegally when they were minors. There isn't a single person in town that'll rat this place out.

In Beaumont, when you have a six pack of bottles, there's only one place you go to drink it—the water tower—and hopefully Liam wins his legal battle against the city to keep it up. Otherwise, where will we go? Or rather, where will the kids go . . . because this place is for them. At least, that's what us old asses keep telling ourselves.

I'm not surprised to see Liam's truck when I pull in. In fact, I'm happy he's here. I have to talk to him, man-to-man, something we've never been able to do. Honestly, I think he still wants to pound my head into the ground because Josie and I were together, and Noah calls me Dad. Thank God for Noah or I'd be dead.

"Liam!" I don't yell his name but say it loud enough he should hear me. If I know him at all, he's rolling his eyes and cursing under his breath. He hates me. I get it.

"What do you want, Ashford?"

Yep, totally hates me. But he likes my son and that's what is important.

I climb the ladder and sit down next to him.

"To what do I owe the pleasure?" he asks.

Instead of answering, I pop the top on a bottle and hand it to him, and then after opening one for myself, I take a long pull off mine. I have no idea where to start. "Josie called. She said Mack is welcome to come to Vermont after Christmas."

"He is."

I don't think Liam knows how much that means to me. Or how much it means that I've had a relationship with Noah for all these years. Losing Josie was one thing, but losing Noah . . . I don't think I would've been able to handle it.

"That's good. Mack will like that." I clear my throat.

"Is everything okay?"

I slowly shake my head and take another drink. Tears threaten to emerge, and I fight to keep them at bay. I'd rather jump off this ledge than cry in front of Liam Page. Can you imagine? "Aubrey's going to South Africa, and she's taking Amelie with her." As I say the words out loud, I realize how fucked up the situation truly is, and how I'm left with very little choice in the matter.

"Well, if Mack needs to go with you guys, Noah and Paige will understand."

I turn and look at Liam, despite it being dark out. Can he see the pain I'm in? The turmoil? "I didn't tell Josie when she called, but uh . . ." I clear my throat again. "Aubrey's moving."

"Oh."

"I haven't told Noah yet, either. I guess it's odd that I'm telling you first, of all people, but . . . yeah. My wife wants to move back to South Africa. I've known this for a while but sort of brushed it under the rug. Mack is excelling in Beaumont and probably has a chance at a scholarship or two. She wants to take it all away, and I can't have that." There's so much pain in my voice. I thought by saying these things out loud to him, I'd feel some sort of relief, but I don't. "I never thought I would be in this position to have to choose my child over my wife, but here I am."

"And Amelie decided to go with Aubrey?"

Nick nods. "A girl needs her mother. Amelie knows she can come back anytime she wants."

"And Mack? How does he feel?"

"He's hurt. Sad. Angry with his mother that she won't reconsider. He doesn't want to leave Beaumont. I think back to when I tried to do this to Noah, right after you came back, and Josie was adamant they stay. She was right. I want to think I'm making the right decision, putting my son's future before my happiness . . . before my *wife's*."

We're quiet for a moment, likely remembering the time when he came back for Mason's funeral, and everything went to shit.

"Do you think it's easier to decide to stay here with Mack because things are over between you and Aubrey?"

"As much as I hate to say it, Liam. I think you're right. Aubrey hasn't been happy for a long time, and I've ignored it. Hell, we don't even sleep in the same room. Most nights, I fall asleep on the couch before going to sleep in the den."

"Is there anything Josie and I can do for you and Mack?"

I'm about to ask the man who hates me, who would rather see me fall flat on my face, one of the most important questions of my life. "I feel like I need to go with Aubrey and make sure Amelie is settled. I don't want to wonder if where they're living is safe. Do you think Mack could stay with you while I do this?"

"Yes, of course," Liam says without hesitation. "When will you leave?"

"Aubrey wants to leave when the kids are released for

winter break. I know you're leaving early. I'll wait until after Christmas."

Liam shakes his head. "Mack can spend Christmas with us. I think Noah would really like that. I know Paige would."

"Are you sure, Liam? I know I have no right asking you to help us."

"We're family, Nick. As much as I hate it, my son looks at you as a dad. I'll never ask him to stop." Liam does the unthinkable and puts his hand on my shoulder. "Are you sure Mack is okay with missing Christmas with you, Aubrey, and Amelie?"

"He already knows his mom and sister are leaving and wouldn't be here. I think spending the vacation with your family will be a good thing for my son."

"Okay, then. Don't worry about anything where Mack's concerned. You may want to get the address from Josie and send Mack's presents there. If you haven't bought any, give me the list and I'll make sure they're under the tree for him."

I nod and let a single tear drip down my cheek. If Liam sees it, he doesn't say anything. He hands me another beer, and I drink it.

An hour later, he offers me a ride home and I accept.

THE NEXT DAY, the headache is real. I can't remember the last time I was hungover, but here I am, nursing a whopper. My staff calls in their lunch order for Whimsicality and I volunteer to go get it. I have to speak to Josie anyway and I might as well go see her now.

Except when I get here, she's having a conversation

with my wife. I'm about to open the door when Aubrey rushes toward it and pushes it open with force.

"I knew you were fucking her," she says loudly, on the crowded street of downtown.

"Aubrey, I'm here to talk to her about our son spending the holidays with her and to give her some money."

"Just admit it," she screams. "The reason you won't move is because of her. Does Liam know? Maybe I should go find him and tell him."

I ignore the bullshit. "The reason we aren't moving is because our son is in high school," I say through gritted teeth. "Look, I don't know what's gotten into you or why you're crying, but you're making a scene."

"Do you want to know why I'm crying?"

"As a matter of fact, I do."

"Because . . ." She pauses and wipes at her tears. "Because of this." Aubrey motions between us. "I know I asked for a divorce, but I didn't expect it to hurt."

"Then make it stop, Aubrey. Let's go to counseling. We can figure something out. Make more time to travel during the summer when the kids are out of school. You can volunteer and do what you love doing." I step forward and reach for her, and for a second, I think she's going to fall into my arms. Instead, she takes a step back and damn, it feels like a kick in the gut.

"It's not that simple anymore, Nick."

"Why isn't it? We haven't filed anything. All we've done is talk. Nothing is set in stone."

Aubrey shakes her head. "It's not what I want." She turns and walks down the street, leaving me there. In a matter of minutes, the entire town is going to know I'm getting a divorce.

I go inside and Josie pops her head out from around the corner. "Hey."

"I'm sorry you saw that."

"I'm sorry for what you're going through." She motions toward the window. "Whatever that is."

I can't help but sigh. "I told her that Mack is going with you for the holidays, and she instantly accused me of having an affair and said she was going to tell Liam."

"Oh."

"Yeah, no matter what I say, she doesn't believe me. I don't get it. Aubrey's the one who wants to leave, but I'm the bad guy because I won't give up my practice, my coaching job, or yank our son from high school. I'm trying to give him a good, stable life, and she's making me feel like I've done something wrong."

"You haven't, Nick. At least from what Liam said. I just want you to know that Mack is welcome to stay as long as he needs. Don't worry. Our door is open."

I pull the envelope from my inside pocket and hand it to her even though I know she won't take the money. Josie will end up using it on the kids, which I'm fine with. I know she and Liam will take care of my son. I trust them. More than I trust my wife right now.

Josie's staff packs up the lunches and hands them to me. On my way back to the office, the staring and the whispering start. Just lovely.

5

CHRISTMAS MORNING

*O*f all the places we could be, I'm happy it's in Johannesburg and not some remote village, although the people there need the most help. The house my contact at Doctors Without Borders found for Aubrey and Amelie is in a gated community, which was one of my concerns. Had I left it up to Aubrey, they'd live in the village where she plans to work, and this didn't sit well with me. When I leave, I need to make sure Amelie's safe. That she has a car service taking her to and from school, and that someone is home when she is. Unfortunately, that won't be Aubrey. The second we arrived in town her new employer whisked her off to assist with a delivery an hour away. As much as I hate thinking ill of my wife, or soon to be ex-wife, I want our daughter to see how absent her mother is going to be and ask to come home with me.

The rental is a cluster home, and has what Amelie calls the oddest swing set she's ever seen in the backyard. The rooms are nice size. Mack will have a bedroom for when he comes to visit his mom. The cabinetry needs to be replaced and the bathrooms are in desperate need of remodeling, but this is what Aubrey wanted. Actually, no. It's what I required if Amelie was going to live in South Africa. If Aubrey had her way, Amelie would be running barefoot in some remote village. Even though I've done it and it's where I met my wife, it's not what I want for our daughter.

Amelie wants to play out front. She's waiting for her new friend to come outside. I'm homesick, missing my son, and wishing we were back in Beaumont opening presents. Amelie doesn't even realize it's Christmas since she opened all her gifts before she left. Thank God for smartphones and the clock app otherwise I'd be lost on what time it is here when it's nine a.m. eastern in the U.S. I press the video button to call Mack. I expect him to be awake since he's one of those who wakes up at five a.m. on Christmas Day. His phone rings and by the fourth ring I'm about to hang up when his face fills my screen. An instant wave of emotion washes over me. Regret, sadness, and longing. I miss my boy.

"Hey, Dad!"

"Merry Christmas," I tell him. "How's it going there?"

He shrugs. "It's pretty cool. The lodge is huge. JD's a riot. He said I can call him that instead of Mr. Davis. And Mr. and Mrs. Westbury said I can call them Liam and Josie. I never realized how popular Liam's band was until we got there. Dad, the ladies were going crazy, screaming his name. It was sort of embarrassing. I mean, I was embarrassed for the women."

"I'm sure Liam appreciates you taking his side. I can't imagine living like that."

"Yeah. Same with Quinn, too. Only a couple people recognized Noah and that was after someone went gaga for Liam. I never want to be famous."

I laugh. "I hear ya, bud. How's everything else?"

"It's good. We're going on this really long snowmobile ride tomorrow. Elle found a diner but it's only accessible by snowmobile, so we rented some and went there. The food was okay, but the ride was fun."

"Have you opened your presents yet?"

He nods. "Yes, thank you for everything. I don't how you managed to get the Griffey cleats, but I'm so grateful. And of course, the new phone is awesome. Peyton said she'd help me set it up later."

"You're welcome. Did Liam like his gift?" Mack has taken a liking to photography and captured a moment between Liam and Betty Paige. When I saw it, I told him he should print it and give it to them, but Mack had a better idea.

Mack's face lights up. "He loved it. He says he has some camera equipment back home and we're going to look through it when we get back."

"That's great. What else have you done?"

"Lots of snowboarding. We met, like, an Olympic snow-boarder. His name is Rush. He's pretty cool. I think Eden likes him."

"How's Noah?"

"He's good. He plays with the baby a lot because he doesn't want to get hurt. He and Peyton have to leave before everyone else, I think."

"Baby? What baby?" I'm not aware that any of their crew was pregnant. Surely, Josie would've said something, or Paige would've told Mack.

"Uh, Peyton's mom and dad are adopting, but not yet. It's whatever comes first. His name is Oliver. He's pretty cute, and has chubby cheeks. But he cries a lot."

"Yeah, babies do that."

"Where's Mom?"

I should've been prepared for this question, but I'm not. "Mom's working," I tell him. "She should be back in town in a few days and then she can call."

"Doesn't she have her phone?"

"Cell service is spotty at times."

"Where's Amelie?"

"Hang on, let me get her."

I walk back into the house and call for her. "Come outside, please." Service is better outside and too unreliable once I go in doors. "Mack's on the phone."

Amelie beams, which I find funny. Days ago, she wouldn't look at him. I hand her the phone and step back to give her some privacy.

"Hey, Mack. What day is it there?"

"Christmas," he tells her. "So, Merry Christmas."

"You, too. They don't really celebrate it here. Dad and I did presents by ourselves."

"Do you like it there?"

"Oh yes, there's lots to do. Guess what!"

"What?"

"I don't have to go to real school. I'm going to learn with the locals."

"That's cool. I'm jealous."

Amelie giggles. She's definitely going to school at the American International School. This is one thing I won't give in on. Amelie needs an education.

"One of my friends is coming. Here's Dad." Amelie waves and then brings the phone over to me.

"She's already popular," I tell Mack. "But she misses you."

He laughs. "I'm sure she doesn't. At least not yet. It's like she's on vacation."

"That's true."

"I should probably go," he tells me. I want to ask him what he's doing or why he has to get off the phone, but I don't. I have to trust that Liam and Josie are treating him as their own and have set some rules down for him.

"All right, well tell everyone I said hi. I'll call you in a couple of days."

"Okay. Hey, Dad?"

"Yeah, bud?"

"When are you coming back?"

"In a couple of weeks. I need to get your sister registered in school and make sure she has a nanny available."

"How come Mom doesn't take care of her?"

Good question. "Mom's going to be busy working. There will be times when she can't come back to where they'll be living right away. Besides, whoever we hire will be able to help with your sister's homework and dinner."

"Then why doesn't she just come back with you?"

I do my best to keep my expression neutral. "She wants to try living here with your mom. We'll come visit though. Once baseball season's over."

"Okay."

"Is Noah around?"

"Yeah, one second." Mack drops his phone and then yells for Noah. "Dad wants to talk to you."

I smile at Mack's use of the word "dad" when he talks to Noah. When Liam returned, I thought I'd lose the boy I had raised. I wish Aubrey could see how much she was a part of bridging the gap between Josie and me, when it came to Noah. He taught me how to be the father I am today. His face and torso appear on the screen and Peyton waves behind him.

"Merry Christmas, Nick."

"Merry Christmas," I tell her. She steps out of the

frame, but I can hear her talking to Mack. She's so loving and caring, treating him like he's part of her family. I suppose with Mack's connection to Noah, he is.

"Merry Christmas, Noah."

"Thanks, you too. How are things?"

I shrug. The truth of how things are, are for another time and place. Not Christmas morning. "Things are . . ." I pause and search for the right word. "Unexpected."

He nods, as if he gets it, which he absolutely does not. What he and Peyton have is one of a kind. I saw it when they were little. Their bond was immediate and unwavering.

"Mack filled me in a bit," he says. "I'm sorry to hear about all of this."

"Yeah, me too. I'm just thankful for your parents. Them helping me with Mack right now is a huge relief."

"You know I'll help him in any way I can. He's always welcome at our place," he tells me.

"I know, but I'll be home soon. Just have to get Amelie settled in school and then I'll be back."

"This is going to be hard for you," Noah points out.

I nod. "That's the understatement of this year and next. But what can I do?"

He shrugs.

"Anyway, I wanted to wish you a Merry Christmas."

"Merry Christmas. Don't hesitate to reach out if you need anything, especially with Mack."

"I will and hey, good luck through the playoffs. I'm so proud of you."

Noah beams. "Thanks. I'll give you back to Mack."

Before handing the phone to Mack, Noah pulls him into the screen. "Take a pic," Noah says. Before I do, I call

Amelie away from her friend, which is almost like starting a nuclear war.

"Come here and smile for a second."

She says hi to Noah and then Peyton, then finally, we smile, and I press the button to take a snapshot. I already know this is going to be my new phone screen saver. Noah hands the phone to Mack after saying goodbye again.

"All right, go have fun, bud. Merry Christmas."

"Merry Christmas, Dad. Love you."

"Love you, too." I do my best to keep my expression happy but I'm dying on the inside.

I wait for the screen to go black before putting my phone down. My heart's heavy and in pain. I'm torn in two. I want to be with my son, celebrating the holidays, but I can't leave my daughter. The fear of not knowing how things are going to go weigh heavily on me. She's not like Mack. He's resilient, a go-getter. Amelie's so dependent on her mother, it's not funny. Granted there's a slight age difference between them, but at ten, Mack had a good head on his shoulders. If someone told Amelie she could fly like a bird, she'd try it without weighing out the consequences.

Staying in a chair in front of the garage, I watch Amelie learn how to double Dutch jump rope. I remember girls doing that when I was in elementary school, and I guess I always thought it was something every girl learned. Amelie tries, fails, and gets frustrated. There isn't anything I can do to help her, and I don't know if Aubrey knows how to do it.

She comes toward me, pouting.

"It's not easy," I tell her. "We can watch a video on it later if you want."

"Can you do it?"

"Nope," I say, shaking my head. "But by watching those girls, I can tell you it's all about coordination. Your eyes have to watch the hands of the person you're facing while your feet do the jumping."

"I can't do it." She crosses her arms over her chest and lets out a huff. "It's not fair."

"You have to practice, Amelie. Not everything's going to be easy in life."

Amelie sags against me. I pull her onto my lap instead of going inside. "Where's Mommy?"

"At work." She knows this.

"When is she coming home?"

"I don't know, kiddo."

"Can I call her?"

I shake my head. "You can, but you'll have to leave her a message. Chances she has cell service where she is are slim."

"Daddy," she whines.

"Not much I can do about it, but it's something you have to get used to," I tell her. "There are going to be days when your mom doesn't come home until after you're asleep, or not at all. Tomorrow, we're going to go visit a service that'll help us find a nanny for you."

"I don't want a nanny."

"Then you have you to come back to Beaumont with me, Amelie. You can't stay here by yourself and you're not going to go live in some remote village. It's not safe."

"How come you don't stay here. You can be a doctor here, can't you?"

"I can, but I need to go back to Mack. He's with Noah's parents right now until I get you settled, then I'm going back. I'll come back and see you in about six weeks, but Mack won't come until after he's done with baseball."

"That's forever."

"I'm sure it does seem like a long time for you." It's going to feel like an eternity for me.

Amelie lays on me, with her back pressed to my chest. She's a wiggle worm and pushing on all my sensitive organs.

I tap her side. "Come on, let's go find some dinner."

"Can we have rice and beans?"

I nod. "Yeah, I'm sure we can find some rice and beans."

We lock up the house, climb into my rental, and head out to find dinner. All the while, I'm hoping she realizes life isn't going to be that great here.

6

New Year's came and went, as did every nanny Aubrey and I interviewed. Well, I did most of the interviewing because she was busy, but nonetheless, we are still without someone to care for Amelie when Aubrey is away—which is way more than she said it would be. Not that I can do anything about that since she wants to live her life—a life with our impressionable daughter at her side.

Thankfully, Mack understands why I have had to delay my trip back to Beaumont. Not that he cares much at the moment. Not with Liam stepping in and filling the void I left. I'm trying not to be jealous, but it I can't lie, it hurts to know how easily adjusted my son is. Or maybe he's only telling me things are okay, so I don't worry. I miss him, but the worrying is at a minimum. I know he's in safe, capable hands, and Liam and Josie are treating him like their own. Josie even sends daily videos, even though I talk to Mack every morning before he goes to school.

Still, it's not enough and I want to get back. Preferably with my daughter but Aubrey fails to see that Amelie being in Johannesburg isn't what's best for her. And it's honestly not best for Aubrey. I'll be happy when she wakes up and sees the damage she's doing to Amelie.

After dropping Amelie off at school, I head to another meeting at another agency in hopes of hiring a caretaker. This will be my third agency. The first person we hired worked for two days, and on the day I was set to leave, she quit. The job was too hard. We hired another from the first agency but they didn't show up. It's pretty much the same bullshit from the next agency.

"Mr. Ashford?"

I stand when my name's called and follow the woman through the open door and down the hall. She points to a chair inside a small cubicle and introduces herself as Sar Newell. Sar types on her computer, asks what Aubrey and I do for work, and then asks me what we're looking for.

"Someone dependable, who drives. They don't need a car as we'll provide one. We'd prefer them to live in the home, but elsewhere is fine as long as their time is flexible. My wife is a nurse with Doctors Without Borders and currently working in Tshwane. There will be times when she doesn't return and whoever we hire will need to stay the night."

"And what do you do for work?"

"I'm a pediatrician, but I live in the U.S. I'll be returning home as soon as possible."

"You're not a doctor here?"

"No, at one time I was, but I live in the States."

She frowns and continues to type. "I have three women who suit your needs."

"Great." That's a relief.

"Come back in one hour. They'll be here for you to meet and talk with."

I extend my hand and shake hers. "Thank you."

As soon as I'm in the car, my phone rings. "Nick Ashford," I say when the number doesn't look familiar.

"Nick? How are you doing? This is Kirk DeBartolo. I heard you were back."

I groan and tap my hand against the steering wheel. DeBartolo was my boss when I did my stint with Doctors Without Borders. He was angry when my contract ended and I wouldn't renew, but I had just married Aubrey and I wanted to get back to my practice. Plus, we wanted to start a family, and that wasn't something I wanted to do in a remote village with questionable resources and no viable drinking water.

"Hey, how are things?"

"Good, could always be better. So, it's true, you're back?"

"No, not really," I tell him. "Aubrey's here working. I came with her to help get her settled."

"You're not staying?"

"Nope." I shake my head even though he can't see me. "Our sixteen-year-old son is still stateside. As soon as I hire a caretaker for our daughter, I'll be heading back. I was hoping to be gone already."

"Ah, bummer."

"Why, what's up?" As soon as the question is out of my mouth, I regret it. I know what's coming and I'm not looking forward to it.

"We're short staffed and could use someone as skilled as you."

"I wish I could."

"The money's good, Nick. Better than it was the last time you were here. And with your experience, you'd have your pick of locations."

"It's not that I don't want to help, Kirk. It's that I can't.

With Aubrey staying here, someone needs to be back in the states with our oldest. He's staying with friends right now and I don't want him to wear out his welcome."

"I understand. Let me know if you change your mind, though. Like I said, we need someone with your expertise, Nick. Especially with children."

And there it is, the knife to the heart.

"Yeah, thanks for calling." I hang up and toss my phone onto the passenger seat. DeBartolo couldn't get me with money, because let's be honest, no one works with the program to get rich. The program is privately funded or done so with donations. Most of the time, doctors use their salaries to buy supplies for patients because there is never enough. But the kids—that's where he gets me, because healthcare is inadequate, and where there's a high rate of tuberculosis and HIV where we are. With the right medicine and treatment, one is curable and the other can be maintained.

I push the conversation out of my mind. There's no way I can do it, not for another two years, and honestly, I'm not sure I want to do it. I love my practice and my staff, and I love watching my patients grow from tiny little humans to rambunctious toddlers to moody teens. I've built a strong foundation in Beaumont and I'm not about to throw it away.

A quick glance at the clock tells me it's time for me to return to the agency. I check in at the front desk and wait for Sar Newell. When she opens the door, she motions for me to follow her. We go to a room, where a young woman sits on one side of the table.

Sar conducts the interview, asking the basic questions, and then I get to ask mine. We do this three times, and then I decided on an unmarried woman in her forties, named Talisa. She doesn't have children and has been a caretaker before. She also doesn't have a problem staying at the house when needed and doesn't need us to provide her a car even though it'll be there for her if and when she does need one.

Finally.

Now I can make arrangements to go back home.

After my interviews, I stop and pick Amelie up from school. She's not a fan because it's nothing like her mother promised, and she hates wearing a uniform. Also, being the new girl is hard work, according to her.

"How was school?" I ask as soon as she comes out of the building.

"I hate it."

"Want to go home?" I ask her this every day or every time she tells me she hates something here. It's probably a shitty thing for me to do but I don't want her here. She needs to be with her brother, back at her old school, and in her room where all of her things are.

"Yes, I'm tired."

Wrong kind of home. I don't correct her as I hold the back door open for her. She crawls in and tosses her backpack on the seat.

"Why can't I sit in the front?"

"Same rules apply regardless of where we are."

"Dumb."

So is living here, but I don't say that to her.

"I hired a caretaker," I tell her as soon as I'm behind the steering wheel. "I think you're going to like her."

"Why can't you stay with me?"

Because you want to stay with your mother.

"I can, in Beaumont, Amelie. That's where my job is."

"Tashia's dad is a doctor, and he works here."

"I'm sure lots of your classmates have parents in the medical field."

"Her mom is in the government. I think she's a spy."

I fight hard not to roll my eyes. Amelie sees one show about an American spy working for the government and now everyone is. Including the President and First Lady.

"You probably shouldn't say that out loud to anyone," I tell her as we turn to head home. "Some people take that word very seriously and it could cause them a lot of trouble. You remember in the movie what happened, right?"

"Yeah, they kidnapped her family."

"Right, you wouldn't want Tashia kidnapped, would you?"

"No, that would be scary, and I'd be sad."

"Let's try and keep our government conspiracies to the house, okay?"

"Okay."

We pull into the driveway just as Aubrey's being dropped off after being gone for two days. She looks haggard and doesn't wait for Amelie or me to get out of the car. I try not to let that bother me, but it does. I get not waiting for me, but to not wait for her daughter? I don't care how exhausted she is, Amelie should come first.

Except deep down, I know she doesn't.

Amelie and I get out of the car and head into the house. I can faintly hear the water running in the bathroom and figure Aubrey's taking a shower. After getting Amelie set up at the table to do her homework, I make my way down the hall and knock on the bathroom door.

"You okay?"

"Not really," she says loud enough for me to hear.

"Can I come in?" I expect her to yell or bite my head off for being intrusive, but she says yes. Opening the door slowly, mostly out of fear she might throw something at me,

I peek my head around the door and find her sitting against the tub, which is filling with water.

I step inside and sit opposite her. We know from experience this job is hard, and after a few weeks of it, the evidence is written all over Aubrey's face.

"Wanna talk about it?"

She shakes her head slowly and wipes away tears from her dirt-stained face. "She was ten. The same age as our daughter. Gang raped and held until she went into labor. They dumped her in the village last night. We did everything we could."

"I'm sorry, Aubrey."

"She was just a baby," Aubrey cries out. "She kept asking for her momma, but we didn't know where she was from so no one could find her. I held her so she wouldn't be alone and told her that where she's going, no one would hurt her again."

"The fetus?"

"Not viable. Her cavity was riddled with sexually transmitted infections and diseases. Neither of them stood a chance."

"You can only do so much, Aubs. You know this. You're there, you're working and teaching these young women how to care for themselves."

"And who teaches the men, huh? Who teaches them right from wrong? Who teaches them not to rape?" Her voice raises and I shake my head slightly, hoping she understands that Amelie can hear her.

"I don't know," I say quietly.

"She was Amelie's age, Nick. Just a baby who needed her mother, and she wasn't there for her."

"Do you know her mom's name?"

Aubrey shakes her head. "She didn't say. Or she didn't

know." She pulls her knees to her chest. "Does Amelie know our names?"

Her question gives me pause. I've never thought about whether Amelie knows our names or not. She's rarely away from us, but Aubrey's question has me thinking.

"I honestly don't know but I'll change that now."

Aubrey stands and reaches for me. I let her even though it'll break my heart. She wraps her arms around my waist and rests her head on my chest. I inhale deeply and then relax before pulling her closer and resting my chin on top of her head. I don't know how long we stand there, just holding each other, but it's enough for me to question whether we're making the right decisions about our lives together.

7

The phone rings with Mack's ringtone and his face fills my screen. I can't help but smile at the photo of us, with him in his football uniform and me holding the trophy our team won when he was in junior high. I realize I should probably update it, but it's one of my favorites of us. I press the accept button and wait for our video chat to connect.

"Hey, bud," I say when I see him.

"Hey, Dad. How's it going?"

Not well. Any and everything continues to circumvent me from leaving here and returning to Beaumont. "It's good," I lie. It's probably the biggest lie of my life right now. Mack angles the phone differently and right away I can tell where he is and I'm both jealous and hurt. I should be there, with Noah, when he takes the field for his first ever Super Bowl. But I'm not. I'm still in Johannesburg.

"Oh, you know. Living someone's dream." My sarcasm is lost on Mack, and I know better than to dump my problems on him. "Are you having fun?"

"So much fun," he says. "Noah brought me into the

locker room and Peyton arranged for a tour of the entire stadium. Liam's going to sing the national anthem."

"Is he? Wow, that's pretty damn special."

"Noah and I wish you were here."

"You have no idea how much I want to be there, bud."

"I get it," he says. "Mom needs you."

She does. At least that's what she tells me. Ever since she had a young girl die on her, Aubrey hasn't been the same. When I told her I had a flight back to the States, she panicked and asked for a few more days. Those days turned into weeks, and each time I bring it up, she tells me she's not comfortable with me leaving yet. I can't tell if it's a ploy on her part or if this is her way of rebuilding our relationship. Most nights, she's made it home either by dinner or in time to tuck Amelie in, and then she asks me to sit at the table with her while she eats. I don't push her, but if she wants to reconcile and fix what's broken, I'd like for her to say something.

"Do you have good seats?"

"Yep, fifty-yard line. We have this huge section because the players' wives are going to sit with us. Grandma Bianca is coming. Josie says I can't listen to anything she says because she cusses like a sailor. It's not like I'm a child and haven't heard someone swear before."

"Do you swear?" I ask him.

"Uh . . ."

I laugh. "It's fine, Mack. I think everyone swears at your age."

"Yeah, we do. It's a thing."

It is. I remember being the same way, although I didn't much care for swearing.

"Do you know when you're going to be home?"

"I'm hoping it will be soon."

"Yeah, but I don't want you to leave if Mom or Amelie needs you. Like, I'm okay with the Westburys. They're really great people. Liam has me pitching to him every day. He taught me how to throw a slider. It's pretty wicked."

And there it is—what I feared most—Liam raising my son. I know some would argue I did the same thing with Noah when he was young, but the circumstances are different. We didn't know where Liam was, and Liam didn't know that he had a son. I want to be in Beaumont. I want to be with both my children. With my family. Together, in one place. But right now, I can't, and short of splitting myself in two, I won't be able to until I know exactly what Aubrey wants to do. This trip was supposed to be temporary. I should've been back by now, but here I am a world away from my son, who doesn't seem to need me. Yet, I need him. I'm not mad at Liam. He's doing exactly what I asked and what he promised. I'm mad at myself. At Aubrey. At life.

"If I remember correctly, Liam and Noah could both throw a nasty slider. I'm happy Liam showed you."

"I like him. He's fun to hang out with."

"And Betty Paige?"

Mack's cheeks flare red. I groan. I didn't have *the* chat with him before I left, and I should've. Adjusting, I inhale deeply and prepare myself. "Listen, I need you to promise me that you're abiding by Liam's house rules. You and Paige . . . well you're too young—"

"Dad," Mack interrupts. "I follow all the rules, and while I like Paige a lot, I respect Liam and Noah. Noah told me she's off limits. I'm listening to him."

"Thank God," I mutter under my breath. "Listen to Noah!"

Mack laughs. "Don't worry. I wouldn't want Liam to

lock me in his basement or anything. That place is soundproof."

"Probably best," I tell him.

"Are you working with Mom?"

"No, but one of my former coworkers offered me a job. I turned it down though."

"Why? You like helping people."

"I do, but I also want to come home to you. If I have a job, I have to sign a contract. Doing so limits my ability to leave when I want."

Mack's quiet for a moment. "I think you should work, Dad. You're a good doctor and things are going really well here. Noah said if I can't stay with his parents I can stay at Peyton's grandpa's. I've been mowing his lawn, too. I miss you, but I also know the people over there would benefit from someone like you."

"I miss you too, bud. You have no idea how much. I'll think about what you said though, because you are right, I do like helping people. However, it's a decision I can't make without consulting Josie and Liam. Maybe even Noah. This is one of those moments where it takes a village to raise a child. They're the village and you're the child. I can't dump you on them anymore than I have."

"Dad, they make me feel like I'm part of their family. I don't know how else to explain it and I'm being respectful. Liam and Josie have rules and I follow each one. Liam's great. We do a lot of things together, especially when it comes to football and baseball. They always make sure my homework is done, my grades are good, and there's always food on the table. I know this was a hard decision for you, but I love you for it. Dad, Noah's about to run out and I don't want to miss it."

"Go, Mack. I'll be watching!"

"Love you," he says as he hangs up.

He hangs up before I have a chance to say anything else. I don't know how long I hold the phone, but it's long enough for my hand to cramp. Quickly, I log into the sports app and project the image to the television. I'm in time to see Liam sing the anthem. What an honor it must be for him to sing before his son takes the field.

Tears spill onto my cheeks and I can't shut them off. I'm bitter. Angry. I *should* be there. Noah worked hard to get where he is and I was there every step of the way, from Peewee to junior high, high school to college when he didn't have any offers for football, only baseball. He didn't give up and walked on at Notre Dame, only to be offered a scholarship the next year due to his performance. I was there on draft day, sitting at the table with Liam and Josie, and I should be at the stadium now, cheering my ass off when he runs out onto the field. But I'm here, a million miles away, torn between my wife who either wants a divorce and doesn't want me around, or is asking me not to leave because she's not entirely comfortable with her schedule yet. And then there's our children. One living his life and telling me to stay and help the people of South Africa. And the other is fighting me every step of the way when it comes to wearing a damn uniform to school and not understanding why it's not safe for her to go to work with her mother. That child has no idea what it's like when you leave a civilized city.

Aubrey comes into the room. I wipe my tears and avoid looking at her. She sits down next to me, too close, but I don't dare move a muscle. I never know when it's going to be an all-out fight which I'm definitely not in the mood for or a love fest.

"What are you watching?"

"The Super Bowl."

"It's so late. Do you need to watch it now?"

"Yes, I do." My words have bite. "Noah's playing." I can barely say those two words without my voice cracking. "It's the biggest game of his life and I'm not there."

"And that's my fault?"

Yes and no.

Yes, because I'm here and don't have the balls to leave. Mostly because of Amelie and there's a silver hope that my wife wants me, that she wants to make our marriage work.

No, because when we left, we had no idea Noah and the Portland Pioneers would crush their competition in the playoffs. They're the underdog. No one expected them to be there. Certainly, not me. If I had, I wouldn't be here.

"It's no one's fault," I tell her. "They won and made it. They could've easily lost." Had I gone home when planned I would've been there.

"Is Mack there?" she asks.

"He is. He called earlier but I thought you were asleep, or I would've taken you the phone. He was in the locker room, and he got a tour of the stadium."

"They're treating him well."

"Like he's theirs," I remind her.

"Are you going to stay up and watch the game?"

I nod and she sighs.

"Okay, well, I'll make some snacks then."

Aubrey heads into the kitchen and returns after the coin toss. She has a bowl of popcorn, chips, and a couple of drinks.

"We don't have much for snacks," she tells me.

"The grocery stores are a lot different here," I point out.

"True." She sets the bowl of popcorn between us and

hands me a drink. "Go Noah," she says as she taps her drink to mine.

Mostly, we sit in silence—that is, until the Pioneers score. Then we erupt in applause, we dance and high-five each other. This is the Aubrey I'm used to. Not the one who emerged a year ago, the sullen withdrawn one. The one who told me she felt suffocated in our marriage. The one next to me is acting like my best friend and partner.

When the fourth quarter starts, we're on the edge of our seats. The score keeps flip-flopping. We're up, then the other team, then us. It's too much and I'm nervous. At one point, I stand and began pacing only for Aubrey to encourage me to sit back down.

"He can't see or hear you," she reminds me. "Sit down so we can watch together."

I do as she says, and she puts her hand on my leg. *Do I ignore it being there?*

"Even if he doesn't win, it's an accomplishment being there."

"I know," I tell her. "But to Noah and the guys, it'll be the biggest let down of their lives if they don't win. Some teams have all the luck and make it to the big game multiple times. Some teams go and don't ever win. And then some teams make it once and never go back. You play to win, always."

"Winning isn't everything," she says.

I give her a sideways glance. "When they're little, yes, because we want them to learn the fundamentals. When you get to high school, college, and the pros, winning is everything. Winning gets you noticed. Losing gets you fired or benched. These organizations are paying their players millions of dollars to win. They're expected to win, and if they don't, they're expected to fix their shit before the next season starts."

"Ugh, that's too much pressure. Oh look, there's Noah."

The camera steadies on him as he talks to his coach. I wish I could read lips to figure out what they're saying. Now I know what Aaron Burr felt like when he just wanted to be included. It sucks knowing the only reason I'm not there is because I've excluded myself. I'm failing Mack as his father, and I've failed Noah.

When the clock winds down, more tears stream down my cheeks. Aubrey's cheering, but I'm dying a little on the inside. The boy I raised, the boy Mason and I taught how to play football, the boy I coached from the time he was little through high school just won the Super Bowl, and I'm half a world away because I can't seem to leave my wife, even though she doesn't want me.

8

*A*ubrey comes into the kitchen, dressed in a pair of navy-blue scrubs, and rummages through the refrigerator. She either doesn't see me sitting at the table or she does and is choosing to ignore me. The latter would suck because as of late, things have been good. We haven't fought, we've enjoyed each other's company, and she's been somewhat affectionate toward me. Those moments are really what sends me into a tailspin. It's like my wife is slowly coming back to me, and I'm not sure what to do about it.

With her head deep into the opening, she says, "Can I make you something?"

So, she did see me.

"I'm good," I tell her. "Coffee's fresh."

"Thank you for making it."

Another new development from her—she thanks me for everything. Thank you for taking Amelie to school. Thank you for doing the laundry. Thank you for leaving a light on for me at night. Her kindness is what made me fall in love with her in the first place and only disappeared a year ago. I wonder what happened that turned her against me and made her jaded toward our relationship. I've spent a few nights staring at the ceiling trying to rack my brain, searching for any incidents, but come up blank each time. Everything seems gradual. Like we both stopped trying somewhere along the way because we fell into a routine. I never stopped loving her but maybe I stopped telling her or showing her. I can't remember the last time I took her out on a date or did something romantic for her.

Fuck.

Aubrey makes herself eggs and brings the plate over, along with a mug of coffee, to the table and sits next to me, not across from me. I'm slouching and trying to adjust without calling attention to myself, but the chair is rickety, as is the table, and I end up jostling it enough that her coffee spills over the edge. I'm out of my seat before she can say anything.

"I'll take care of the spill," I tell her. I'm back with the pot and a towel to clean up the mess I created because she makes me feel awkward. It's like we're dating all over again and haven't been together for the past twenty years. "Sorry about that."

"Accidents happen."

After taking the wet towel to the sink, I rinse it out and set it on the side to dry. "What time are you going to work today?" Normally, she's gone by six in the morning, if not earlier.

"A little later," she tells me. "Jacoba had to take Hanneli to the doctors this morning and I didn't want to ask you to drive me out there." Jacoba is the other nurse Aubrey works with. She lives down the road from us and her daughter, Hanneli, often plays with Amelie after school.

"Is Hanneli okay?" Immediately, I wonder if I should've noticed something when I saw her the other day.

"Yes, as far as I'm aware."

"That's good." Guilt weighs heavily on me about being here and not working, and also being here and not in Beaumont. Amelie isn't adjusting well and has gotten into trouble at school. Ideally, Talisa would be the one to pick her up, but the one time we tried that, Amelie threw a fit and I had to get her anyway. It seems to me my daughter is doing everything she can to keep me here.

"We need to talk about me heading back to Beaumont," I say to Aubrey. She looks up from her eggs, in mid-bite and stops chewing for a second. "I know things are going well, but we need to think about our son. I was supposed to be back by New Year's, and then it was another two weeks, then the end of January. We're now almost to the end of February. It's going to be spring break soon."

"But—"

I hold my hand up. "I know, your schedule is wonky, and Amelie is . . . well for a lack of better words, being a troublemaker. Which I absolutely don't like, Aubrey. She's acting out because of the situation, and we shouldn't tolerate it."

"What situation?"

I do everything I can not to be sarcastic or raise my voice. *What situation*? I must be the only one living in reality while Aubrey floats from cloud to cloud in Lalaland.

"Our *situation*." I emphasize the situation because I really don't know where we stand on the whole divorce thing. She hasn't brought it up since we arrived and I definitely haven't pushed the issue, despite my attorney calling to see if I've received the papers he emailed. I have and I don't like them. Ashford v. Ashford—dissolution of marriage —really hits you right in the gut when you read those words.

Aubrey puts her fork down and takes a sip of her coffee. And then another sip. She holds the mug in her hands, and I wonder if she's going to hurl the ceramic object at my head because I'm not exactly being forthcoming with her.

"I don't understand why you want to go back to the States, Nick. In the time we've been here, things have been good."

Except they're not.

"Our son is there, Aubs. And I know you're tired of hearing this, but we can't take him out of school. He's doing well and has a bright future ahead of him. Imagine if we did and he struggles like Amelie. She's miserable and acting out, which isn't good for her. Or us. We have to discipline her for a situation we put her in. That's shitty parenting. You promised her this really cool life, when in reality, what you're doing is dangerous and not safe for her. How would you feel if she had seen the girl her age you had to treat and lost? Those are horrors I'd like to keep out of her life for as long as possible."

"The schools in the states aren't much safer."

"I'm not talking about the schools. I'm talking about how hard the adjustment has been for her. If you tell me she needs her mother, and her mother wants to live here, then you need to be home for her, every night. You can't depend on Talisa to raise Amelie."

"I'm not," she says quietly.

With some hesitation, I place my hand over hers, expecting her to pull it out from under mine. She doesn't and a smidge of hope surges. "I need—" I'm cut off by my phone ringing. I glance down at the screen and frown at the unknown number.

"Nick Ashford?"

"Nick. Kirk. How are you?"

"Fine." I pinch the bridge of my nose and sigh, DeBartolo hears me and grasps my annoyance with him.

"I ran into Aubrey the other day. She says you're still in town."

Funny, Aubrey doesn't want to look at me right now.

"Yep, for a bit at least, still ironing out some details."

"I could use you for a consultation downtown. Won't take but an hour or two."

Don't ask him what he needs.

Do. Not. Ask.

"What's the problem?" I ask, knowing I shouldn't.

"Not a problem, per se. I have a presentation this afternoon and I could really use someone with your knowledge and experience to help me push for more funding."

"That's not really my thing," I tell him. "I'm in private practice for a reason."

"Aubrey mentioned that."

"Did she now?" She still won't look at me. "I didn't know you went out to Tshwae to see patients."

"Oh, I don't. She was downtown."

"I see."

Aubrey gets up from the table and takes her plate to sink. I watch her like a hawk, wondering what else she's keeping from me.

"Look, Nick. I'm not going to beat around the bush and use some board meeting to entice you to come downtown. I need your help. Your skills are useful and needed here. The salary offer is double. The job is yours. Let me know, okay?"

"Yeah." I hang up and stare at my wife's back. "Aubrey."

She visibly stiffens and then turns slowly.

"Did you have lunch with Kirk DeBartolo?"

She nods. "He said he had an offer for me, so I met him. Turned out to be a pitch on how to get my husband to come back to work for him."

"I see." I say again, because it seems to be the only answer I can give that won't give away my frustration or disbelief.

"The money's good, Nick."

"I make more back home," I tell her.

"But here, you'll be helping people who need help. Who don't have access to first world health care. Who can't afford a doctor like you."

"Our son—"

"I get it," she interrupts me. "He can't leave, and you need to go back. Or you stay and you work here, and we work on us."

"Aubrey, are you asking me to choose you over our son?"

"Yes." Then she shakes her head. "No, I'm not. I don't know what I'm asking, Nick. What I do know is, I love being here. I love helping, despite the horrors I've seen. Amelie will learn to love it once she finds her groove."

Aubrey steps forward, closing the gap between us. "And I know you feel it, the shift between us. Since we've been here, we've been different. We're not fighting. We're happy. I know you miss practicing, helping people. Being kind is in your nature and it's eating you up on the inside to sit here all day long with idle hands when you could be helping."

She comes closer.

"And you already said Mack told you to work here."

"It's not up to Mack," I tell her. "We are relying on people to take care of our son. A woman, I might add, you accused me of having an affair with not too long ago."

"I was angry."

"You were angry?"

She nods.

"So, you lashed out at a married woman and threatened to tell her husband a lie? People we consider our friends?"

Another nod. "Should I call and apologize?"

"Absolutely, yes," I tell her. "Josie didn't deserve you saying those things to her. Neither did I. I've been nothing but faithful to you, Aubrey. I wish you'd believe me."

"I'm trying. I really am, Nick. I know I said some really hateful things and honestly, I expected you to leave me, but you didn't and you're still here. It makes me wonder if we have something worth saving."

I pull her into my arms and hold her tightly. Leaning back slightly, I lift her chin with my index fingers so I can look into her eyes. "We do, Aubrey."

She rises on her toes and pulls my head down toward her. Our lips brush against each other's. Hesitantly, at first and then she opens for me. The moment our tongues touch, it's like a kaleidoscope of colors bursts through my mind. Everything around me seems vibrant and shiny, and powerful. I pick her up and her legs wrap around my waist as I head toward the bedroom. Only for my phone to ring. If we were anywhere else, I'd let it go to voicemail.

Groaning, I stop in the hallway and Aubrey slides down slowly, bumping my erection on the way. This time I moan. It's been over a year since we've had sex, and I've missed my wife terribly.

In three big strides, I grab my phone from the table and see Liam's number on my screen. Instant panic arises. I press the button and wait for the video to connect. "Is Mack okay?"

"Hey, yeah," Liam says. "Sorry, I should've texted you but uh . . . I signed Mack up for a recruiting program and I wanted to fill you in. The band shot a music video the other day and I had the videographer put some content together of Mack, and I sent it off in hopes of getting some scouts out here to see him pitch."

Relief washes over me. "He said you taught him how to throw the slider."

Liam nods. "He's a natural, Nick. We should be thankful we didn't have to play against him in high school. I don't think anyone is going to hit him this year."

"That's fantastic." I am dying inside because, once again, I feel like I'm failing my son as it's not me who's signing him up for recruiting programs.

"Anyway, you're going to get a shit ton of emails because I put your email in there as well as mine. Anything he gets from a scout or recruiter, you'll see. Just email me what you think and we'll go from there."

"I can't thank you enough," I tell him. "How's Mack doing in school?"

"Thriving," Liam says proudly. "He's doing well, Nick. You've raised an outstanding young man. He's been helping out at Mr. Powell's, mowing his lawn, washing the car that rarely moves, and going to the grocery store for him. I've been teaching him to drive, if that's okay. I probably should've asked first."

"No, that's perfectly fine. We were going to do that after football and then. . ." I trail off. "If I need to sign anything, email me and I'll take care of it."

"Everything good there?"

I turn, only to find Aubrey gone. My hope is she's in the bedroom, ready and willing to pick up where we left off. Looking back at Liam, "I've been offered a job here."

"Mack mentioned that after the game. You were really missed."

Heart meet knife, twist.

"I hated missing it."

"So, are you going to take it?"

"My son—"

"Your son is doing well, Nick. We love having him, and if the time comes when we don't, we'll let you know. If you need to stay because of your family, do it. But do it knowing Mack is being taken care of. Things are good in Beaumont," he says. "I'll have him call you when he gets home from school. We're going to the batting cages after dinner to hit some balls under the lights. He said he struggled with that last year."

"Yeah, he did. Thanks, Liam."

Liam sighs. "You did it for Noah, Nick. I'm just returning the favor. Mack will call you after school." He hangs up before he can see me lose my shit. I don't know whether to scream or cry right now.

Or both.

I move about the house, looking for Aubrey. Because if it isn't my heart aching for my son, it's because my wife just left without saying goodbye.

9

*I*f it wasn't for Liam and Josie, my life would suck even more than it does now. I accepted the job, but not without conditions. I'm never out of town and I start after Amelie's at school. Talisa picks Amelie up every day, however, I've gotten into the habit of taking her and it's not something I care to stop.

I have never hated my profession, until now. It's not the patients or the work, it's the demand. There aren't enough of us to go around, and those of us who are around, are already spread thinly. We are pulled in every which direction, with a mountain of work waiting for us. Being here makes me miss my private practice even more, and even though I love practicing medicine, this isn't where I want to be.

Which means while Aubrey and I are trying to reconcile, or I'm trying to make things as perfect as possible for her while she continues to send me hot and cold messages, I'm encouraging her to think about heading back to Beaumont. Where she works is dangerous, riddled with situations I don't want her to be in. At night, I worry about her safety, about when she'll be home, or worse, whether she'll even come home.

And when she is here, she's absent or aloof, especially when something terrible has happened at the clinic. I get it, losing a patient really knocks the wind out of you, even though you always tell yourself not to get attached. It's hard not to, though, when you know you're fighting a losing battle even though you've told your patient's loved ones you'll do everything you can. Most of the incidents that rock her to her core have to do with young women, mostly around Amelie's age. Those nights, Aubrey comes home and cries for hours. Angry, hot tears, and a verbal barrage of words thrown at me because I'm there. I'm her punching bag. Not because I deserve it. Aubrey has amazing parents who guided, nurtured, and taught her everything she needed to know to survive. The young women Aubrey treats are naïve, lost children of circumstance, whether it's because their parents have passed away or they simply can't take care of them. By the time they make it to Aubrey or any of the other staff, it's usually too late. Disease riddles their bodies, making it impossible to treat. The ones the staff can catch early, those are the success stories. Those are the nights when Aubrey comes home happy and smiling.

I miss that smile. I miss seeing the corner of her lips crinkle or her eyes widening with happiness. Now when she does smile at Amelie or me or Mack when she's on the phone with him, it's short lived. This tour she signed up for, the place she wants to live, is draining the life out of her and she's too stubborn to recognize it. If I bring it up, I'm harping. Sometimes, that's all I do—harp. I can't help it.

As soon as I walk into the house, I inhale cinnamon, garlic, and turmeric and sigh. One of the best things about Talisa being Amelie's caretaker is the magnificent food she makes for dinner. I go into the kitchen, set my bag on the chair, and make my way over to the stove to breathe in the Cape Malay curry. It's one of my favorite dishes. Talisa likes to spoil me.

"Wash," she says as she shoos me away from the stew. I love having her around, she keeps our house in order and us well fed. Honestly, I'd like for her to come and live with Mack and me in Beaumont when I go back, but I need her to stay with Amelie.

I do as she says and then stop in Amelie's room to check on her. I find her at her desk. It's a small wooden desk Talisa found on the side of the road. She repaired it, painted it white, and added flowers for decorations. Amelie's head is down, and her shoulders are shaking.

"Amelie, what's wrong?" I step in and place my hand on her shoulder. "Why are you crying?"

"Because I missed Rachael and Ebony's birthday parties and now, they don't want to be my friends." The last part comes out in a sob and my heart breaks for her. She hasn't had the easiest time making friends at her school and really only plays with Jacoba's daughter, Hanneli. But even Hanneli has her long-time friends who aren't that interested in Amelie. It makes sense though, most of the Doctors Without Borders families are in a place for six months to a year, so why get attached.

I sit on the edge of her bed and run my fingers over the fringe on the bedspread Talisa gave Amelie. It's different shades of reds, oranges, and pinks, and reminds me of the sunset. "Do you want to talk about it?"

She shakes her head and turns to face me, hair covering her face. Tears trickle down her cheeks and she wipes them roughly. "I want you to tell their parents that they have to be friends with me."

I shake my head slowly. "Friendships don't work that way, Amelie. They don't have to be friends with you if they don't want to. I'm sure if you were in Beaumont, things would be different, but you're not there and they're ten years old."

"They're eleven," she says.

Semantics.

"It doesn't matter. I'm not telling their parents they have to be friends with you."

"You're so mean."

"I'm fully aware," I tell her, which only angers her more. Man, I love the little girl attitude. "Is there anything else bothering you?"

She nods and does another swipe across her face. "I'm sad."

"I can see that. Would a hug make things better?"

Amelie shakes her head. "I miss Mack."

"Me too, sweetie. So much."

"Make him come here."

"I can't do that. Mack's at an important stage in high school. If he moved here, it would ruin his chances of going to college."

"He doesn't need to go to college. He can sell stuff on the corner like the other kids."

There's a lot to be said about living in a small-town, especially one that prides itself on taking care of their neighbors. Beaumont doesn't have an issue with homeless people since the town pooled its resources and bought the hotel on the outskirts of town. If someone needs a place to stay, there is always room, and someone always has odd jobs available if they need money. Leave Beaumont and it's a different story, much like every other town or city's story. There aren't enough jobs, housing is outrageously overpriced, and the cost of living is through the roof. Our economy is slowly forcing people onto the streets. What Amelie sees are people on the streets, selling their goods in hopes of putting a meal on their table at night.

"Mack needs to finish high school and go to college. The same will be said for you."

Amelie groans. "I hate school." She comes over and falls into me. I have no choice but to catch her before she dramatically slides to the ground. I pick her up and sit her on my knee.

"What else is going on?"

"You'll be mad."

"I doubt it."

"I thought it would be fun to live here but I miss my old room and my friends, but I like Hanneli and I really love Talisa. And Mommy is here."

Mommy can go home, too.

"I know," I tell her. "I miss a lot of things back home, too. Maybe we should talk to Mommy about all of us moving back."

Amelie rests her head on my shoulder and grows quiet. I hold her, swaying back and forth, taking in the moment before the attitude returns.

"Daddy?"

"Amelie?"

"I want to go home."

"Okay, baby."

That night, after we've called Mack and tucked Amelie in, Aubrey and I crawl into bed. It's been baby steps, but we're at least sharing a bed now. And while I'd love to be making love to my wife every night, our sex life hasn't returned. We had a week of rekindling sex, but by the next week it had tapered off and I'm back to feeling like a stranger in her life. I know she's tired and her mind races with the horrors she's seen during the day, but being intimate, being taken care of, should assuage those thoughts.

I lie on my side, with one hand under my pillow and the other in the middle, hoping she grabs it and pulls me to her. I have no choice but to let her lead, let her dictate how things are going to go. The rejection stings.

"Aubs?" I say her name in the darkness.

"Yeah?"

Finding the words to bring this up are hard. I start to question myself, wondering if there was a time before we crawled into bed that I could have dropped the bomb our daughter isn't happy and wants to go home.

"When I came home from work, Amelie was crying in her room. She told me she hasn't got any friends and asked me to call some parents and tell them their kids have to be friends with her. She told me she's not happy here, Aubs."

"She's ten," Aubrey says. "She'll adjust."

"That's not fair."

"Why isn't it, Nick? If we had moved for your job or sold our house and moved to a new town, she would've had to switch schools. The same shit would be going on."

Aubrey has a point.

"You're right. I'm sorry."

The bedside light switches on and Aubrey sits up. Even though most of the light is on her side, I can see her glaring at me. Slowly, I sit up and mentally prepare for the fight we're about to have.

"I'm sorry," I say again. "When I saw her like that, I

should've thought of how things could very well be different if we had moved for other reasons."

"Right, but you blamed me instead."

"I didn't blame you for anything."

"Right. I'm sure you told her that she needs to hold her head high and face adversity, to put herself out there and try to make new friends, to maybe go to the dance class she wanted to take or stay after school and do one of the programs."

Aubrey looks at me pointedly.

"No, I didn't. I wasn't thinking about those things. I saw the tears—"

"And made me the bad guy."

"That's never my intention, Aubrey."

"Look, I know you didn't want this. In fact, I didn't ask you to come. You came because you don't trust me, which really sucks, Nick. I'm a good mother. I've taken care of my kids from day one, while you worked long hours and rebuilt the practice you gave up because Josie broke your heart. I was there, remember? I picked up the pieces. This is what I want. This is where I want to be. I don't understand why it's such an issue."

"Aubrey, I never said you weren't a good mother, but come on, what am I supposed to think when you tell me you plan to live in the village and not send Amelie to school?"

"That's how I grew up."

"Things are different now," I tell her. "The world is different now. You sprung all of this on me, weeks before Christmas. And I'm sorry, but this could've waited until the summer. Hell, we could've had a long conversation and planned things out, but no, it's what you wanted and now here we are. Our family is a mess. Amelie's not happy.

You're not happy with me." I take a deep breath. "I'm not happy."

"Then leave, Nick. I don't want you here." She gets out of bed. "I don't need you."

Not—I don't need you *here*—it's I don't need *you*.

"Just get out, Nick! I'm so sick and tired of you being in my space. I want you gone. Leave!"

"Mommy," Amelie's voice sounds small, scared.

Aubrey turns slowly and looks at our daughter, standing in the doorway. I get out of bed and rush to her, scooping her up in my arms. Amelie cries in the crook of my shoulder. "Come on, let's get back to bed." But Aubrey isn't having it.

"Nick, I want you to leave."

If this were any other time, I'd go. After setting Amelie down on her bed, I turn and slowly walk until Aubrey has no choice but to back up.

"I'm not leaving Amelie. If you can't stand being in the house with me, you can go. We can figure out the rest tomorrow."

"There's nothing to figure out, Nick. I want a divorce."

I smirk because there it is again. When shit gets tough, she bails. "You can have it, Aubrey. I'm done trying with you." I don't wait for her response and head back into the bedroom to grab my shit and take it to the guest bedroom. As much as I want to slam the door, I don't. She doesn't need to know she's gotten to me.

I walk back to Amelie's room, making sure she's tucked in and do my best to assure her everything is going to be all right.

Even though I don't believe a word of it myself.

10

The couch I sit on is puke green and being propped up in one corner by a couple of books. The fabric is rough and not something you can relax on or take a nap. It came with my new apartment. Only there isn't anything new about this place. It's old, outdated, and not at all where I want to be. But I did what Aubrey asked and moved out. It's what she wants, and while it's not what I want, I'm done fighting with her. I can't take the hot and cold, the wishy-washy feelings. She wants a divorce, so that's what I'm going to give her.

Amelie comes out of her new room, hands on her hips, and a look of distaste on her face. "I don't like it," she tells me.

"I know." It doesn't matter where we live. It'll never be home. As far as I'm concerned, this place is temporary and the sooner I can get out of my contract, we are out of here, the sooner we can be back in Beaumont. Well, I will be. I can't stay here. It's not for me and as much as I want my daughter to return with me, she wants to stay with her mother. I get it, but don't like it, and want some strict custody arrangements before I leave. Right now, Amelie will stay with me for the next couple of days and then she'll be with her mom.

Staring at my daughter, I never thought I'd be in the situation I am in now. None of this makes sense. I'm ridiculously angry at Aubrey for leading me on and letting me think we were going to work things out. It's clear she never had any intentions of doing so and led me to believe we could because she needed someone to help with Amelie. I'm not sure I'll ever be able to forgive her. My heart isn't broken, it's numb. I've lost all sense of feeling when it comes to my wife . . . well, now soon-to-be-ex. Tomorrow, we'll meet at some mediator's office, who doesn't know us or anything about our marriage, and go over the paperwork my lawyer sent us. There isn't a doubt in my mind, Aubrey won't like the agreement, but I have a feeling she'll sign it because she wants out.

After dinner, Amelie takes a shower and then joins me on the couch. I put a blanket down so our skin isn't scratched by the fabric. As much as I don't want to, I'm going to have to find a better place to live or do some remodeling here, the latter depending on if I can work out a way to finish my contract early or not. Who thinks of sitting on a couch when looking at a rental? Definitely not me but then again, until we arrived here, I hadn't rented anything in decades.

"I don't understand why you couldn't stay at the other house too. There was an extra bedroom."

Amelie shouldn't know any of this, but she does. She heard the last fight Aubrey and I had, and it all started because I brought up how Amelie wasn't happy. Truth is, the only one that is happy is Aubrey and that's questionable half of the time.

"It's fine," I tell her. I'm determined to make this work. It's not like I can walk away from my responsibilities. It's not in my nature, no matter how badly I want to leave. "We can make some changes, maybe buy a new couch."

"Okay," she says as she snuggles into me.

We watch a show until she's yawning and dozing off. After tucking her in, I boot up my laptop and read over the divorce decree. Ashford v. Ashford feels like a knife in my heart. I had hope. I thought once we were back here, things would be different. Aubrey would see that we belonged in Beaumont and suggest we go back. Instead, she kept renewing her six-week contract, even though she came home in tears most of the time.

Nicholas Ashford retains full primary custody of minor children: Mack and Amelie. Mr. Ashford will provide health insurance for the minor children and pay two-thirds of Amelie's care while living with Aubrey Ashford. Mr. Ashford will pay for a full-time caretaker while Amelie is in the care of Mrs. Ashford. In lieu of spousal support, Mr. Ashford will pay the fee on the rental home, as long as Amelie is in the care of Mrs. Ashford. Payments will cease when Amelie returns to the United States.

While in the care of Mrs. Ashford, Amelie will attend the International School at the expense of Mr. Ashford.

At the time of this decree the extracurricular activities Amelie participates in are as follows: Dance. Foreign Language Club. Soccer. These expenses will be covered by Mr. Ashford. Any changes to activities will require Mr. Ashford's approval. If Mrs. Ashford wishes to add an activity, it will be at her expense.

The residence in Beaumont, as well as the private

medical practice will remain with Mr. Ashford. Within one year from the date of the dissolution of marriage, Mr. Ashford will refinance the home and bequeath one-third of the profits to Mrs. Ashford. The remainder will go into a trust for the minor children.

After a while, the words blur. I can't believe this is what my marriage comes down to—words on a piece of paper—dictating what I'm going to pay so Amelie isn't struggling. It's a crap shoot that Aubrey's going to sign this. Something tells me she wants money. Aubrey wants a divorce, not a trial. A judge here can only issue spousal maintenance. My lawyer is banking on Aubrey signing and walking away.

I'm not sure if I expect her to fight me for custody. I don't want Amelie staying with Aubrey for the foreseeable future, but I will listen to what my daughter wants. After all, her happiness is what's important here. I am willing to concede and let Amelie stay as long as she wants. Last week, she didn't want to stay. This week, she does. I expect she'll change her mind again, and again.

The entire thing makes me sick. I hate that my family is torn apart, that I failed at keeping it together. It's the worst feeling in the world, hearing your wife tell you she wants a divorce. What's worse is the way she looked at me when she said it. Any love I thought we shared was gone. The thing is, I don't know where it went because weeks ago, she told me she wanted things to work between us.

What changed?

I close my laptop, turn off the television and make my way into the small bedroom that'll be mine until I either find another place or my contract ends. Part of me is willing to suck it up. I'm only here to sleep and I don't need much so I'll put up with the twin bed that's situated in the far corner. Amelie, however, deserves a better place to live in.

Then again, Aubrey wanted her to live in a village. The divorce decree will prevent that.

Outside, lights shine into my window from people coming and going. I stare at the ceiling. There are patches of plaster. Holes filled in, but not sanded or painted. Just globs of white cement all over the ceiling, waiting to fall down on an unsuspecting sleeping man. Sort of like my life.

AFTER WORK, I head to the mediator's office. I'm not sure how my attorney found this place, but they are willing to be the go between with my lawyer. With my hand poised on the door handle, I glance across the street and come to a sudden stop. My wife is there, in the arms of another man. He hooks some of her hair behind her ear and stares down at her tenderly. When he leans down and kisses her, every part of me is torn. Do I say something or ignore it?

I say nothing as I walk into the office. She doesn't want me, and I shouldn't care. Except I do because I want to know how long she has been with this man. From what I saw, they looked comfortable with each other, and people who just started dating don't normally express themselves with a lip lock on the street. They don't engage in PDA or give loving looks to each other. Not to mention, it's been a week since we called it quits for good. Did she really move on this fast? I'm trying not to let what I saw sting, but it does. I am only human after all.

Aubrey walks in, straightening her hair as she comes toward me. Her lips are red, and I know it's from being kissed. I've seen them enough to know. She sits next to me and has the nerve to smile. I smirk and think about when it'll be the perfect time to bring up what I saw.

The mediator calls us into the small, cramped office. It's too close for comfort and I want the door to stay open for air flow and a quick escape when Aubrey starts with her crocodile tears.

"I'm assuming you've looked over the decree?" the mediator asks.

I nod and Aubrey sighs.

"Yes, and it's not okay," she says. "I need spousal maintenance. I haven't worked much during the marriage and don't have any assets."

The mediator nods.

"You have a job that pays you two thousand a month, no bills, and I'm paying your rent."

"So?"

"Okay, the alternative is I don't pay your rent and you can have it in spousal maintenance."

"You're only willing to pay as long as Amelie is living here."

I shrug. "And I'm going to refinance the house. You get one-third of the profits." A house she paid absolutely nothing for because when she was working, she sent her money to her parents. I never told her otherwise because I knew it was important to her.

"Maybe there's another solution?" the mediator asked.

"There has to be," Aubrey says. "I have to have income to live."

"You keep one hundred percent of your earnings, Aubrey. I'm paying for everything for the kids. Healthcare, education, extracurricular activities, and a caregiver, which wouldn't be needed if we were living back in the states."

She looks at the mediator as if they should say something. The settlement is more than generous considering the circumstances.

"You just want to be back there because of Josie," she mumbles. I don't know if she didn't expect me to hear her or what, but I did and use it as an opening.

"Who is the man I saw you kissing?"

Aubrey looks at me with fake confusion on her face.

"Don't, Aubrey. I saw you across the street. It wasn't some friendly peck on the cheek. Who is he and how long have you been seeing him?"

She says nothing. Her silence hits me straight in the chest. It's not that she thinks I've been cheating, it's her, I'm sure of it. I'm sure of it.

"How long, Aubrey?"

"It doesn't matter."

I scoff and wish we were anywhere else having this discussion. "It matters. Did you break our family apart and move across the world for some guy you met on the internet? Or do you know him from when you lived here?"

She stares at the mediator, who is looking down at the papers on the table.

"Take the offer, Aubrey, or I'll push this further."

"And when you take Amelie from me, then what?"

I shrug. "That won't be my problem. I'm willing to pay for your rent while she is with you. When she tells me she's ready to go home, which I know she is now, we're gone."

"You promised me Mack would be here."

Another shrug. "He's old enough to make his own decisions about where he wants to live. Right now, he's thriving in Beaumont. I'm not going to allow you to interrupt his life anymore."

It takes a while, but Aubrey nods. The mediator says they'll have the final paperwork ready for us to sign in a couple of days. I'm out of my seat and the office as fast as I can move. There isn't a need or desire to stay in Aubrey's presence anymore.

"Nick!" Aubrey screams my name as I head down the street. I stop and turn.

"What?"

"You really think it's okay to screw me over like this?"

"I did no such thing, Aubrey. The deal is fair."

"When you take Amelie, I won't have the money to pay rent."

"Then move," I tell her. "Find a smaller place or ask your *friend*. I'm sure he'll help you. Better yet, ask your parents for all the money you sent them during our marriage. I can add that you worked and never added to the household income. You don't think I have those records?"

"Why are you being such an ass?"

"Because . . ." I point my finger in her direction and then shake my head. "You lied, Aubrey. I don't know when you started, but I'm sure if I go back and start looking at things, I'll be able to figure it out. You lied to me. To us. To our children. It's all starting to make sense now, the sudden urge to move. You put yourself before the kids and that'll never be okay with me."

"You drove me into the arms of another man."

I hang my head and groan. "You're right," I say. "Treating you like you were the best damn thing to ever happen to me, worshiping you, putting you first . . . yep, I'm the bad guy here." I start to turn away but have more to say. Facing her, I say, "I never cheated on you. I never even looked at another woman. From the moment I met you, you were it for me. My life. You did this, Aubrey. You chose this for yourself."

She stares, saying nothing.

"I don't know who he is but keep him away from my daughter."

"You can't tell me what to do."

"I just did. And don't even think about asking her to lie to me, Aubrey."

With those parting words, I walk away.

11

When I get back to my new, outdated apartment, my mood isn't any better. I'm angry, pissed off, and frankly, exhausted from feeling all those things. Yet, no matter what I do, my ex finds a way to twist her serrated knife a little bit more, to make me feel pain I never thought I'd feel. I open the refrigerator and wish beer would appear. I haven't bought any because I don't want to give Aubrey ammunition to use against me in any proceedings.

"He drinks in front of Amelie." My mind changes her voice from the one I love—well loved—to some nasally whiny nails on the chalkboard sound. She's never sounded like how I'm imagining, but she needs to in my mind right now because hearing her voice still sends a fucking jolt to my system.

Loved.

Who am I joking? I still love her and probably will for some time. But I can't think of anything but her kissing that man across the street. It wasn't a friendly kiss. Not like the kisses she gave me weeks ago. No, that was a thanks for rocking my world, can't wait to see you tonight kiss. I know those kisses. I've lived with them for many, many years.

Now, I live with nothing but painful memories that my mind keeps telling me have been filled with lies and deceit. How has she moved on already? I find it impossible, unless he's the reason she's moved us here.

No, she didn't move *us*. *She* moved here and demanded her children come with her, because no matter what, at the end of the day, she's a mother, and a damn good one.

I moved here out of my own selfish need. I wanted her to want me, to see that she needed me, but she didn't. Aubrey placated me until she'd had enough.

But then . . . why make love to me? Why tell me she wanted to try and fix things?

None of it makes sense, and I don't think I'll get an answer out of her any time soon. She knows cheating is a hard limit for me.

Nope.

Just like now.

"Ugh," I push my hands into my hair and tug on the ends, pulling until my scalp screams and burns. Honestly, that feels better than the giant hole in my chest does. I look down, expecting to see a red spot or blood oozing from the gaping wound left by Aubrey.

Another flash of her and the man across the street.

They'd definitely been together, I surmise. The way he tilted her head back with the lift of her chin. The way he brushed her hair out of her face, curling the loose strands behind her ear. Her breasts, full and voluptuous, pressing into his chest while her fingers toyed with the waistband of his pants. I can only imagine her smile. The same one she'd given to me for years she now gave to someone else.

I take my phone from my pocket and dial the director of

my program. He begged me to come back, to be on staff, and I reluctantly agreed knowing I needed an out when things went south. They are as far south as they're going to get in my opinion.

"Nick, what can I do for you," Kirk says when our call connects.

"I need to get out of my contract," I tell him, only to realize I should've started off with some elaborate excuse, like my mom's sick or my house flooded. Neither of which are true, and ideas I don't want to put out in the universe. Mostly because I hate lying about situations that could come true. Honesty is the best and only policy. Deep down, this is something Aubrey and I should've practiced a year ago when she began to turn my advances away. Instead, I retreated to the office and slept on the couch. That was my mistake.

There's a long pause, followed by a sigh. "I can't do that, Nick."

Somewhere, deep in the recesses of my mind, I knew this. "I don't need the money," I tell him. "I'll pay back what you've given me."

"Nick, it's not that. We need you. Now that you're signed on until November, others are heading home to see their families. I can't tell them they can't go."

I pinch the bridge of my nose, knowing full well I should've never agreed to this. "Things aren't good for me here," I tell him. "Aubrey and I—"

"I heard," he says. "Honestly, I was a bit surprised by the whole thing."

"Yeah." I was but wasn't. It's not like she didn't tell me she wanted this months ago.

"I guess I didn't realize you weren't together when you moved here."

"I didn't move here . . ." His words give me pause. It wasn't necessarily what he said, but how he said it. "What do you mean?"

"Just that I'm surprised she's engaged. She came into the office the other day, flashing a ring around. From what Jokoba says, they've been together for a year now."

Everything in me dies. Every. Single. Part.

"Nick?"

"Yeah, I'm here."

"I'm guessing you didn't know she was engaged?"

I clear my throat. "Kirk, up until a few weeks ago, we were still fucking. Hell, technically, we're still married until the divorce papers are finalized. So no, I didn't know my wife was having an affair." I hang up. Talking to him isn't going to get me anywhere. Only after, do I realize I should've left my dirty laundry in the hamper and not shared it on the clothesline.

I'm pretty certain I pace a hole into the floor of my apartment. The downstairs neighbor probably wonders what I'm doing to make the floor creak. I know I'd be fearful that the ceiling was going to fall in with how rickety everything feels.

The alarm on my phone sounds, it's time to pick Amelie up from school. On the days I have her, I like to give Talisa time off. She's still paid, but I want to be more hands on. On my drive, I think about how life is going to be when I leave here, how things are going to be for Amelie. Will she solely depend on Talisa or will Aubrey be as present as she was back in Beaumont. I really want to know what she's thinking or if she thought I'd find out.

Should I say something to her?

Every fiber of my being wants to ask her what the fuck is going on. I feel as if I'm owed an explanation. Do I want to hear about her affair? No, I don't. I don't need the details. Just the why. Why not just leave me? Us? Why the big song and dance?

I slam my hand against the steering wheel in aggravation. The more I think about the situation, the angrier I become. What's the point? She's likely to lie or tell me it's none of my business when I think it is.

Did this man come to Beaumont?

Was he in our home?

Our bed?

Around our children?

Amelie comes toward the car, with a bright smile on her face. I know I'm going to tell her before I can even think about the pros and cons. She *has* to know, mostly for my own peace of mind.

"Hi, Daddy," she says as she climbs into the back. "How was your day?"

"Hey, sweetie." I steer the car back into traffic and turn toward the apartment, thankful it's a five-minute drive. "How was school?" I ask, avoiding her question.

"Meh," she says shrugging. I catch the act in the rearview mirror and smile. She's animated, adventurous, and temperamental. The latter comes with age and I know she'll grow out of it. Damn it, I'm going to miss her, and hate the idea of leaving her. I don't care if I have months left, leaving her behind is going to destroy my soul.

Amelie catches me staring and gives me a wide, beautiful toothy smile. I love her more than my own life. Her and Mack. My pride and joy. The best parts of me.

I park and help her out of the car, carrying her backpack. She leads us upstairs and waits for me to unlock the door. For everything she's going through, she's managing well.

"Can I watch TV?"

"How much homework do you have?"

"Some reading and spelling words."

"Let's do that first, and then you can watch TV while I make dinner."

"Can we call Mack?" she asks as she empties her backpack onto the table. I look at the calendar app on my phone and see that he has a game.

"Probably not," I tell her. "He's got a game, so he'll be busy after school."

"I miss him."

"I know. Me too."

Beyond measure. Being separated from him is the worst feeling in the world.

I help Amelie with her homework. We run through her spelling words, mastering them by the third try. She sets off to the living room to watch her show while I whip us up something to eat. After dinner, she showers and then joins me on the couch.

"I want to talk to you about something," I tell her. She sits crossed legged in front of me, with the most serious ten-year-old expression she can muster. "It's adult stuff."

Her nose crinkles. I can't say I don't blame her.

"You know Mom and I love you very much, right?" She nods. "And you know we're not going to live in the same house anymore, right?" Her happy-go-lucky expression changes. The sadness in her eyes breaks my heart.

"You're going back to live with Mack, aren't you?"

I shake my head slowly. "Not right away, but yes, I will. Your mom wants you to stay here with her, and Mack needs to stay in Beaumont. But once he's done with high school, I'll move back here with you. Okay?"

Amelie nods, but the smile doesn't return.

"Some more adult stuff," I tell her. "I want you to know, that if there's ever a situation that you don't like or you need me, I'm only a phone call away." I hold my phone up. "There are going to be some changes in your life and they might be hard to deal with. You may not like them." Lord knows I don't. "And well . . ." I'm suddenly at a loss for words. How do I tell my impressionable daughter that her mother is marrying another man?

I don't. It's not my job. It's Aubrey's.

"Just know, I'm always here. I don't care what time of night it is or whether you think I'm sleeping. If you need me, you call me."

"I don't have a phone," she whispers as if I didn't know this.

"You will tomorrow. I'll make sure of it." And tomorrow, when she goes to her mom's I'll take her because Aubrey owes me an answer or two.

My phone rings. Josie's picture fills my screen. I accept her video call and wait for it to connect. "Hey," I say as soon as I see her. "Where are you?"

"Hi Amelie," she says before addressing me. "Mack's pitching. I thought you'd like to watch the game."

My heart swells with adoration for the woman on the other side of the phone. I'll never forgive myself for making things difficult for her when Liam returned. It's hard watching your family slip away knowing there isn't anything you can do it about. Sort of like now. Except, this divorce business with Aubrey is different. I'm not losing my kids, just my wife. A wife who truly doesn't want me anymore.

"Thanks, Josie."

Amelie sits close to me as I hold the phone in front of us. Josie turns the camera toward the field and there's my son, wearing the same number I did when I played. Mack stands on the mound, ball in one hand and his mitt resting on his thigh. He's waiting for the okay to start, to stare the batter down. I've been there before. Same with Liam. Then Noah. And now Mack.

"Hey, did I miss anything?"

I hear Noah's voice. Tears threaten to spill, but I fight them back. He leans in front of the phone and waves.

"Hey, Dad," he says, catching me off guard. My breathing hitches and I'm thankful he can't the quick intake of breath.

"Hey, Noah. How's it going?"

"Great."

"Hi, Noah," Amelie waves. I think she has a crush on Noah. And Quinn. And, my luck, JD.

"Yo, Amelie. What are you doing, beautiful girl?"

Suddenly, she's bashful and giggling.

I hear, "Play ball," and my anxiety skyrockets.

"Steeeerike," the ump says. Josie and everyone cheers Mack on and I fist pump.

The first three batters strike out. The first half of the inning is over. Josie gives me a play by play of who is batting and what's going on.

"Mack's up," she says. I can faintly see my son coming up to bat and then the phone's jostled.

"Sorry," Liam's voice calls out. "She's trying to show you this shit through the fence. I moved you for a better shot."

"Thanks." I clear my throat, moving the frog size lump away from my windpipe.

The view is clear. I see my son step into the batter's box, with the bases loaded. He lets the first pitch go by, ball. But the second, he sends it over the fence for a grand slam.

"Holy shit!" I'm jumping up and down, forgetting about

the weak floors. Yelling for Mack, right along with Liam and everyone in the stands. Liam's the loudest, rooting for my son, the boy he's taken under his wing and helped shine.

I stay on the phone, watching the entire game, long after Amelie's fallen asleep on the couch next to me. When it's over, Liam hands the phone to Mack, whose smile beams from ear to ear. Someone, I'm assuming Liam or Noah, messes up Mack's hat. He doesn't care to fix it.

"Dad! I hit a grand slam!"

"You did. I saw it. I'm so proud of you and hey, you pitched a no-hitter. I'm going to need a copy of the newspaper tomorrow. I bet you'll be on the front page."

"Yep, just like you, Noah, and Liam."

"Yeah, you're right."

"I'll make sure Josie saves it for you. I miss you."

"Ah, bud. Not as much as I miss you. I wish I could tell you I'm coming home, but I'm having some trouble getting out of my contract."

"Dad, you can't leave Amelie," he tells me. "She needs you."

I look down at the sleeping beauty next to me, whose feet are awfully close to places I'd rather them not be. I cross my leg, giving myself some protection.

"We'll talk about it later," I tell him. "I'm proud of you, son. So damn proud."

"Thanks, Dad. I love you."

"Love you too, bud."

"Should I call Mom and tell her?"

I nod, even though I want to be selfish. "Yeah, I'd call her. But wait until you get up for school. She's probably sleeping." Or doing things she doesn't want her son to interrupt.

"All right. Talk to you tomorrow."

After he hangs up, I sit there, with nothing but the TV for lighting. We muted the sound hours ago, neither of us caring because Mack was playing. Resigned, I scoop Amelie up and carry her to bed. She wakes, just as I lay her down.

"Daddy?"

"Yeah, baby girl."

"How come Noah calls you Dad?"

I brush her hair away from her face. "Because a long time ago, when he was younger than you, I was his dad."

"What about Uncle Liam?"

I sit on the side of her bed and tell her the story, the kid friendly one where we're all one big happy family.

"That's sad."

"It is, but then I met your mom and we had you and Mack, and I was happy."

"Are you happy now?"

I nod, even though I'm far from it. "I am. Now go to sleep. I love you."

"Love you, night."

"Love you more than you'll ever know." I leave her door cracked a smidge and then head into the shower where I let the tears I've held back all night flow freely.

12

Spring morphs into summer and right before my eyes, Amelie's almost done with school. She splits her time between my apartment and her mother's house, and one night during the week, either I go over there for dinner or Aubrey comes over here for family dinner. I think it's important to show Amelie that her parents are still there for her, regardless of our marital situation.

Aubrey and I are cordial. I don't ask about her day, and she doesn't ask about mine. We don't really talk unless it's about the kids because there isn't anything to talk about. She still hasn't told the kids she's getting married, not that she's told me either, but at some point, she may want to drop the bomb.

I've asked to meet the new boyfriend a few times, but Aubrey never commits to anything. Deep down, I worry. As a father, I want to know who is going to be around my kids. Raising them when I'm not around. Now I know how Liam felt when he came back and saw I was raising Noah. We weren't exactly friends in high school, and it must have been a kick in the gut to see his rival playing father figure. I get it now. I don't want a stranger raising my kids either, simply because they're not *me*. Honestly, I'd like to sit down, see where he stands on some important issues, and go from there. I don't expect us to like each other. Hell, I don't hate him like I should mostly because I have a feeling Aubrey didn't tell him she's married. Every time I think about what's happened, it makes me wonder what else she's hidden from me.

It's sad to think my marriage ended on lies. Lies upon lies. I can't trust a damn thing that comes out of her mouth. Shortly after our first meeting with the mediator, she told me the house needed a new dishwasher, dishes, towels, really trivial things. Aubrey said because Amelie used them, I needed to buy them. At first, I thought I was going to be on the hook, because yes, Amelie does use those things, but my attorney said no. The landlord could cover the cost of the new dishwasher, if they chose, but Aubrey had to fork over her share as well.

For a while I expected things to get messy, but thankfully they haven't. When Amelie's here, we have a great routine. Talisa has started coming over during the week. She cleans, does the laundry, and makes sure the refrigerator is stocked. At times, she cooks, which I fully appreciate. Her food alone is worth what I pay her.

Each day, I go to work, treat my patients with a smile, and count the days until I head back to Beaumont. Mack insists that I stay here for Amelie, but I'm not sure. Besides the fact that my son is living with friends, I miss my practice, my friends, the life I had in Beaumont. Amelie knows I want to leave, but when she's here, we don't talk about it. When all of this started, I said I'd come and get them settled. Somehow Aubrey weaseled more time out of me. I could've told her no, but I wasn't staying for her.

When I walk into the apartment after work, the smell of curry wafts over me. I inhale, loving the scent. I've decided it's my new favorite cuisine and all others pair in comparison.

"Mr. Nick." Talisa comes around the corner, wiping her hand on her towel. "Good evening."

"Good evening, Talisa. Dinner smells amazing."

"Soon," she told him. "Miss Amelie is in her room."

I knock on the door and then open it. She's on her bed, with her headphones on, reading a book. I know, without asking, she has music playing. How her mind can do two things at once is beyond me.

Tapping her on the shoulder, I wait for her to remove the device. "Hey, Daddy."

"How was your day?"

She shrugs. "It's boring sometimes."

Amelie started complaining the work was too easy. Aubrey and I met with the school and asked for Amelie to have the next level of course study, which also turned out to be too easy after a couple of weeks.

"I'm sorry." I sit on the edge of her bed and sigh. "Not sure what I can do to help."

"It's okay. I just get bored."

"And boredom leads to trouble?"

She nods.

"Did you get into trouble?"

Amelie shakes her head. "Not yet."

It takes everything in me not to roll my eyes. "Let's try and stay out of trouble then. Come on, let's eat and then we're calling Mack."

After Amelie and I do the dishes—it's not something I expect Talisa to do—we sit down and call Mack. When he answers, he's smiling big and bright.

"Hey guys," he says. He looks like he's been running around.

"What's going on?"

Mack turns his screen around and shows us a dog, and then he's back facing us. "This is Beau," he tells us. "He's Ben and Elle's puppy. I'm taking care of him and helping train him."

"He's soooooo cute," Amelie says. "I love his name."

"Yeah, he's the sweetest."

"How's Ben?" Liam or Josie keeps me up to date on the happenings in town. I was shocked and saddened to find out Ben had cancer. He's so young and you never think of people his age going through something like this.

"Uh, he's in the hospital," Mack says. "I don't know all the details because I'm just a kid, but he collapsed the other day when he was buying the puppy. I was there and called for an ambulance. Elle's paying me to train him. I pick him up from her studio every day after school."

"You're a good kid, Mack."

"Thanks, Dad. Uh, when are you coming home? I really miss you."

My heart sinks to the pit of my stomach. I need a clone because that's the only option for me so I can be in two places at once. My son deserves to be with his parents, but not at the expense of his future. If he were here, he'd be somewhere in boarding school, and we'd have the same conversation."

"I miss you too," I tell him.

"Do you miss me?" Amelie asks him.

"I do, but your friends really miss you," he tells her. "I see them a lot and they ask about you and want to know why you don't call them. I tell them the time difference is sort of crappy."

"I have new friends," she tells Mack, which irritates me. Her tone reminds me of Aubrey, and I don't like it.

"Why don't you go take your shower," I tell her. She waves bye to Mack and heads toward the bathroom. "About me coming home. I have to wait for a few things to become final here and then I'll be back. Do you want to come here for the summer? I know your mom misses you."

"Does she?" he asks. "She never calls. I talk to you every day."

"I'm sorry, bud."

Mack shrugs. "Liam said he'd take me to look at some colleges this summer. Besides, I'm mad at mom."

Me too.

"She didn't need to go back there. If she wanted a job she could've worked here."

"I know. But this is where she grew up and her parents are here."

"Yeah, the grandparents that never call. I wonder where she learned that habit from."

I don't say anything. He's entitled to be angry with his mother and grandparents. Hell, I am. They don't call Amelie either and when they were in town, she was here. Aubrey never thought to switch weeks. When I asked her about it, she didn't see what the big deal was. Sometimes it's hard to understand why people are different. Being a grandparent is supposed to be the highlight of your life, your achievement for raising your own kids. My parents adore the kids and are extremely pissed off at me for allowing Amelie to move here. If only it was that easy. I get that they're angry. So am I. But being stuck between a rock and a hard place isn't fun either.

"How are your grades?" I ask, trying to change the subject, even though I know he's a straight A student.

"Good. I'm ready for school to be over."

"I used to feel the same way. And then summer wasn't ever long enough."

"Nope." The puppy comes into view, kissing Mack's face.

"He's really cute."

"If you were here, I'd ask if we could get a dog."

"Yeah, we kind of talked about it for a bit but never really did anything about it. I guess in hindsight that's a good thing."

"I guess. I gotta go. I told Mr. Powell I'd mow the lawn and I still need to work on some commands with this fluff ball. Say hi to your Uncle Nick," Mack says in a baby voice. "Noah's been here a lot too."

"That's good. Are you spending a lot of time with him?"

Mack nods. "He did say I could go to his place for the summer if I wanted. He said his dad can be kind of annoying, but I don't think he is. Liam's helped me a lot."

"That's good. I'm happy."

"Yeah, all right. Love ya, Dad."

"Love ya too, bud." Only Mack doesn't hear me because he's ended the call.

I sit there and stew until Amelie's out of the shower. After tucking her in, I head for the kitchen and grab a beer from the refrigerator. When I first moved out, I made sure to keep any alcohol out of the house, out of fear Aubrey would use it against me. At this point, I don't care. And it's not like Amelie is awake to tell her mother, and I'm definitely not getting black out drunk.

After a couple of swigs, I pick up the phone and call Aubrey. She picks up on the third ring, sounding out of breath. Gee can't imagine what she's doing.

"Busy?"

"No," she says, but I can tell she's lying.

"Why aren't you calling Mack?"

"Excuse me?"

"I didn't stumble over my words, Aubrey. Mack says you haven't spoken in a while, what gives?"

"I text him."

"That's not the same. He needs to see your face, hear your voice."

"And he would if you didn't allow him to stay in Beaumont."

"Do you really want to talk about why we're not in Beaumont?"

Silence.

"Yeah, I didn't think so."

"I feel like you're trying to scold me or something, Nick. I'm sorry I'm not as perfect as you when it comes to our son."

"Stop," I tell her. "Stop with the gaslighting. Just call your son. Let him know you're okay, that you're happy. Let him see your life here so he understands why you made this decision without thinking about him."

"That's not fair, Nick, and you know it. You're turning him against me."

"I'm not, Aubrey. We rarely talk about you. If you think he's distant, it's because you're not putting in the effort with him."

"Well, the effort goes both ways."

"Not when you're sixteen and you're navigating life without your parents, knowing they're going through a divorce. Call your son, Aubrey." I hang up, wondering if I've done the right thing. It would be so easy to push this all under the rug, to not encourage her to reach out to him. But I can't do that to Mack. He and Amelie are innocent in all of this. They didn't ask their parents to get a divorce or to move away. Adults making rash decisions and not fully thinking about the ramifications did. I get that Aubrey wants to live where she grew up. It makes sense. And I understand she wants her children or at least one of them with her. I'd want the same, but not at the expense of their happiness.

I finish the beer, lock up, and turn off the lights. In bed, I stare at the ceiling, still waiting for it to fall on me some night. Hopefully, I hear it start to crumble before that happens. Who knows what's up there, living and breeding. The thought makes me shudder.

13

It's Aubrey's week to have Amelie, but instead my daughter and Talisa walk into my apartment. I mute the television and instantly rush to Amelie. I give her a once over, looking for bumps, bruises, or scrapes before asking why she's not with her mom. Believe me, it's not that I don't want her with me because I do. It's more that her mother will have the biggest freak out and she's the one I don't want to deal with.

"Mrs. Ashford has company for dinner," Talisa says. "Ms. Amelie didn't want to stay and asked that I bring her here."

Amelie nods, looks over her shoulder and up at Talisa. "What she said."

"Who's at the house?" I ask.

"Mommy's new boyfriend."

My heart sinks for Amelie, knowing this is the first time Aubrey's brought him over when Amelie's there. I sensed things were moving along and they were ready to move in with each other when she brought a few of my items over that I left there, but I've not actually asked Aubrey if my instinct is correct. I have done my absolute best to stay out of her life, to let her live it, as long as Amelie isn't affected. Honestly, I'm surprised Aubrey waited this long to introduce them. If what my director says is right, they've been engaged for a while and dating well beyond that. Maybe my ex is trying to save face with her daughter.

"Thanks, Talisa. You can go home. I'll take Amelie home later."

Amelie heads right to her room while I walk Talisa out to her car. It's dark and while my neighbor is okay, I don't trust things that lurk around corners. Once Talisa is safely inside her car, I head back in, lock up and go to Amelie's room.

"Wanna talk?"

"Did you know she had a boyfriend?"

I nod, step inside her room, and sit on the edge of her bed. "I did."

"How come you didn't tell me?"

"Well, mostly because it's not my place. That's something your mom needs to share with you and because while I knew, I found out in a way your mom never intended me to and she hasn't confirmed it. So, I really couldn't go around saying something. I take it this is the first time you've met him?"

She shakes her head.

"No?"

"He's been over before, but as a work friend, mom said."

This isn't something Amelie has mentioned, not that she needed to. "What's different about tonight?"

She shrugs and looks away.

"Amelie what's going on?"

"I don't think he knew I was there, and I heard him talking to Mommy in her room. He said, 'did you get rid of the kid yet' and she told him to be quiet, and then he yelled a bit about how he doesn't want kids and she's known this for a long time and how she showed up with one."

Every fiber of my being ignites with fire. I hate her for putting our daughter in a situation like this, with someone like that man. For disrupting our family.

I pull Amelie into my arms and hold her as she starts to cry. "I'm so sorry," I tell her, trying to assuage her broken heart. No one should ever hear those kinds of words from anyone, especially their mother's boyfriend.

"Daddy?"

"Yeah, baby girl."

"Can I live with you?"

My head nods before I can even form the words to tell her she can. I have full custody and have the final decision. For a long time, I've felt the only reason Aubrey wanted Amelie was for money and comfort.

Obviously, it's not something I can prove.

I get Amelie some dinner and then head into my room to call Talisa and ask her to come back. When she arrives, I tell them I'm heading over to get some of Amelie's things and tonight should be like any other night, dinner, some television, and then a shower.

On the drive over, I call Aubrey, but she doesn't answer. I know that someday my mind won't immediately go to what I think she's doing with this man, and when that happens, I'm going to rejoice. Because right now all I can think about is my wife cheating on me while I struggle to find a common ground between being her husband, raising one child here and another back home, and questioning what the hell I'm doing.

When I get to the house, even though I have a key, I knock. And knock. Until she opens the door. Her hair is down and she's wearing one of the kimono robes she loves so much. There isn't a doubt in my mind I've interrupted her.

"Nick, what are you doing here?"

"Where's Amelie?" It's one of those low blow questions, but I want her to think our daughter isn't where she should be.

"I thought she was with you."

"Did you call to check? To make sure Talisa made it to the apartment?"

"No, I—" I brush by her even though I should respect her space. I'm angry, my thoughts are muddled, as are my emotions. "Nick, you can't just come in here."

"I pay the rent on this place." I point out. "And our daughter is at my apartment crying her eyes out because of you."

"Look, I admit I didn't break the news to her that well."

That's when I see it, a diamond engagement ring on her finger. She sees me looking at it and drops her hand.

"I can explain—"

"You really don't have to, Aubrey. We're divorced. You're free to do whatever you want, even though I know you cheated. You know, it all makes sense now that I think about it. You accused *me* to alleviate your own guilt. Pretty clever. What I don't get is why you brought us all the way here."

"What do you mean?"

"Correct me if I'm wrong, but our daughter overheard your *fiancé* ask you if you got rid of the kid yet. Now, being a doctor and a parent, I gotta say that's a pretty big red flag."

"It's not what you think."

"No, then tell me what it is because our daughter is at my place crying. She was so upset she had Talisa bring her over. What do you want me to say to her, Aubrey? Your

126

boyfriend or fiancé doesn't want kids, and yet you have two of them." I begin to pace, pushing my hands through my hair. "You know what this looks like, right? How this feels to her? To me?"

Aubrey stares. Not at me, but down the hall. I follow her gaze and start to laugh. "So, he's here? Hiding in the bedroom, huh? Not man enough to come out to face me."

"Nick, stop."

"Stop? You're serious right now? The only thing going through my mind is you're hurting our kids to please your boyfriend and you want *me* to stop?"

She nods.

"Go get him. I want to meet him," I tell her. "I want to meet the man you destroyed your family for. The man you're willing to give up your children for."

"I'm not giving up my children."

"The hell you aren't. Do you really think I'm going to let Amelie come back here after he made those veiled threats? You didn't even deny them, Aubrey. You let some man tell you what to do with your daughter. She's supposed to mean more than a piece of dick."

"She does!" Aubrey screams and wipes at her tears. "I told him she's not going anywhere. That we're a package deal."

"I'm taking her back to the states."

"You can't do that."

"You know I can. I have full custody of the children, Aubrey. It's not safe here for her. I've said this from the beginning. The only reason she's here now is because I didn't want you to kidnap her."

"Nick," she says my name quietly, almost as if she's shocked, I would say something like that.

I shrug. "When you told me you wanted to move and

take the kids that's the first thing that went through my mind. Everything you've done, you've done so with your boyfriend in mind. You know damn well moving Amelie here wasn't a good idea. You made a selfish decision for a man who doesn't even want kids. Who isn't even man enough to come out here and face me," I say the last part loud enough for him to hear. "That's what you want? A man who doesn't even stand up for you?"

The door to the bedroom opens and the man walks out. Without cars and a busy street separating us, he's a bit shorter than me, a little beefy with no hair. I can't tell if he shaves it or if he's bald.

I look from him to Aubrey, who looks absolutely horrified.

"Aren't you going to introduce us?"

She sighs heavily. "I don't think you'll like the irony of the situation," she says quietly.

"I see. Should I guess?"

She shakes her head. The guy steps forward and I expect him to hold out his hand for me to shake, but he doesn't, which is probably a good thing.

"I'm Liam," he says in an accent so heavy it sounds like his name is lye-em.

Aubrey's right. I don't like the irony. "Really?"

"There's more."

"Can't wait to hear it."

"We were engaged before you came here," she says, which is absolute news to me. "When I met you, I broke it off with him to be with you."

"Oh, you've got to be fucking kidding me, Aubrey. Really? After everything I told you about what brought me here in the first place. You cheated on him with me?"

"And then you with me, it seems."

I glare at Liam, Lye-em, however the hell he says his name. He's no better than her, breaking up our family.

"I can't believe you," I say as I head down the hall.

"Where are you going?"

"To get Amelie's stuff."

"She's not moving with you, Nick."

I turn around and head back to where they're standing and look him dead in the eyes. "Do you want children?"

"Not at all," he says without missing a beat.

My eyes bore into Aubrey's. "I'm going back to the states, and I'm taking Amelie with me. If you want to be her mother, you'll figure things out on this end. I will not sit by and wonder if my daughter is going to make it to my next visitation because her mother's boyfriend doesn't want children. You should've thought about that when you rekindled your relationship with him."

Then I turn to him. "Thanks," I tell him.

"For what?"

"For making it easier to get the fuck out of here."

I take what I can, while Aubrey sits on the couch crying. I fear she's upset because she's going to lose money, not that Amelie is leaving. I tell her I'll be back for the rest of the stuff sometime this week and if she wants to see her daughter, she knows where to find her.

When I get back to the apartment, Amelie's snuggled up with Talisa. I ask her to wait while I put Amelie to bed. "Your mom will come and see you here," I tell her. "We can talk more about it in the morning. But for right now, you don't have to go back to your mom's if he's there."

"Thank you, Daddy."

"I love you, Amelie." I kiss her forehead and turn off her light. Talisa stands when I come into the living room.

"Am I fired?"

I shake my head but also grimace. "My contract is up in November, and I'm going to take her back to the states."

Talisa starts to cry.

"I'm sorry, I truly am, but I have an offer for you."

"What is it?"

"Come with us. I have a son who's sixteen, almost seventeen, and I own my medical practice in a town called Beaumont. It's small, quaint, and we have a lot of friends there. Our house is nicer, you'd have your own room, and I'd double your pay. I need someone to be home with the kids, especially when I'm on call and need to leave in the middle of the night. I know you don't have family here, or not much family, and would understand if you say no—"

"Yes," she says, interrupting me.

"Yeah?"

"I love that little girl, Mr. Nick. I don't want to lose her."

"We love you, Talisa. You're very good with Amelie and I know Mack will love you as well. Fair warning, he's an active kid. He plays a lot of sports."

"I don't mind. Thank you."

We go over some loose logistics and I tell her I'll get the paperwork started on a work visa for her. After I walk her out to her again, I head inside and into my bedroom. Just as I'm crawling into bed, my phone rings with a video call from Mack. I sit up and turn my bedside lamp on and accept the call.

"Hey bud," I say when he comes into view.

"Hey, did I wake you?"

"Nah, just crawled into bed. How are things going?"

"Things are good. But, uh, I wanted to tell you something."

"Okay, what's up?" I try to keep my expression neutral even though I'm shaking like a leaf on the inside.

"Well, I . . . look don't be mad, okay?"

I don't know how much more I can take tonight. "Mack, just spit it out, bud. It's hard for me to be mad when I'm here and you're there. Is Liam mad at you?"

His face blanches. "No, not at all."

"Okay, then. What is it?"

"I took Betty Paige out on a date last night," he tells me. "We went to the movies. I paid for it with the money Mr. Powell gives me for mowing his yard."

My heart goes up and down, side to side, flips, flops, and twists. Not only have I not been there to teach my son to drive, but I've missed his first date. Not only his first date, but one with Liam Page's daughter. My body temperature rises and not in a good way.

"Liam was okay with this?"

Mack nods. "I asked him first," he tells me. "I mean I had to ask if I could go out, but then I asked him if it would be okay if I took Betty Paige to the movies."

"As friends?"

Mack's cheeks flare pink.

"I like her, Dad. A lot, and I know she likes me."

I know. I've known for years.

"Okay." I'm not sure how to proceed. Liam knows so that's good. "Promise me something, Mack."

"Liam already had the talk if that's what you're going to say."

"I wasn't, but that's good to know. Just be careful, okay?"

Mack nods again. "Dad?"

"Yeah, son?"

"I kissed her." He grins and giggles and then the little shit hangs up the phone.

14

*T*iming is everything. If Amelie hadn't shown up on my off week and told me about her mother's boyfriend, whose name I can't even bring myself to say, I'd be sitting alone in my apartment asking myself, "Self, what the fuck are you doing?" I came to South Africa to make sure my daughter was okay, make sure she lived in a safe neighborhood, to enroll her in school, and had a schedule full of activities. Even though Aubrey told me she was going to be around for our daughter, the reality is, she's never here. And maybe that's my fault. Maybe knowing I was here to make sure Amelie was okay made her think she didn't need to be present. Who knows.

What I do know is our luggage is packed and sitting by the door, the car rental returned, Talisa's work visa is approved and in hand, and as soon as Aubrey gets here, we'll be on our way to the airport.

When I first brought up moving back to Beaumont to Amelie, she hesitated. As I knew she would. I'm not trying to take her away from her mother—I'm trying to protect her. The things she said, and the man her mother is choosing to be with, put my daughter in harm's way. I had hoped Aubrey would see the light, but she's in love or re-in love as she's called it and has blinders one. At this point, there isn't any arguing with her. If she wants to see Amelie and Mack, she'll come to the states. If she wants them to come to wherever she'll be living, Talisa will fly with them, and the fiancé won't be allowed anywhere near my children. It's simple, I don't trust him. I've seen enough child abuse victims in my office, true crime documentaries, and stories of parents or stepparents doing the unthinkable to their kids. That won't happen to mine. Not as long as I'm alive.

Aubrey's car pulls up and I usher Amelie and Talisa outside. They each carry a bag, while I make a couple of trips to get everything. Talisa is excited about moving to the states and tells me she plans to watch *Coming to America* on the plane. I don't have the heart to tell her how outdated the original film is, and how where we're going is nothing like Queens. I think she's going to enjoy living a subdued lifestyle and after a week, everyone in town will know her by name.

While I've been gone, Liam has been busy revitalizing the downtown space. He's purchased the building next door to Whimsicality and has turned some of the floor into different businesses, such as a photography and dance studio. There's a new bakery, ice cream shop, and some other businesses. Of course, this isn't enough for him. He decided to start his own record label—FMG Records— whatever that's supposed to mean. Liam's hired Elle to work for him, while she manages her bands. Betty Paige works there as well while Mack works wherever he's needed, which is mostly at Mr. Powell's or walking Beau, Ben and Elle's dog. After Ben's cancer scare, he and Elle have decided to spend more time in Beaumont, which is great for my son because he's very attached to their dog.

Of all people, it was Josie who convinced Amelie to move back. With a new dance studio opening up, she said she'd sign Amelie up for lessons if she wanted. And the owner of the photography studio offers classes. There were things to do now. In less than the year we've been gone, Beaumont has grown. The only thing I cared about was the water tower. Not that I want Mack drinking there, but it's a rite of passage and I'd hate for him to miss out on it. Liam assures me, it's not going anywhere.

When we arrive at the airport, Aubrey pulls along the curb and puts her car into park. She gets out and opens Amelie's door, while Talisa and I gather the luggage. Aubrey and Amelie are hugging, and I can't hear what they're saying to each other. Whatever it is, I'm sure it's not overly pleasant if Amelie's doing all the talking. She's very upset with her mother right now. Can't say I blame her.

Aubrey lets her go, and then comes over to me. She rocks back on her heels, and I wonder what's on her mind. The thing is, months ago, I would've asked her. Now, I don't really care.

"Thanks for the ride," I say. Should I shake her hand? Thank her for almost twenty years of marriage? I'm not sure I'm thankful, not after the things she told me when I confronted her. She never fully loved me, not in the way I loved her. She pined for a man she had given up when she met me, and for what? To go back to him? It's Josie and Liam all over again, and it fucking stings. The difference is, I *knew* about Liam. I knew I was always the second choice in Josie's life and as much as I wanted to be first, I never would've held that title as long as Liam Page was alive.

"That's it?"

"What do you want from me, Aubrey?"

"A hug would be nice or for you to tell me you're sorry for taking Amelie away from me."

I step forward and give her a one arm hug and don't even touch the last half of her request. I'm not sorry. I should've stood my ground from the beginning, but I wanted my family to stick together. At the time, I thought I was doing the right damn thing.

Live and learn.

Aubrey mumbles something unintelligible and I don't care enough to ask her to repeat herself. She goes to Amelie again, and instead of eavesdropping, I start taking the luggage over to the porter. It's much easier than dragging all of these bags through the airport. I hand him our passports, and Talisa gives him hers. Her hands are shaking. Gently, I rest my hand on top of hers to ease the anxiety.

"Everything is good," I remind her. Some of her friends told her it was hard to get into the states and that they'd kick her out as soon as she got to the airport. It doesn't matter how much I reassure her she still looks over her shoulder and shakes like a leaf when she sees the police.

"Amelie, we have to go," I say as soon as the porter hands over my tags.

Aubrey hugs her again, and I can see it in Amelie's eyes, she's not happy. I hold my hand out and she skips over to me.

I'm about to step through the door when I stop and turn. My ex, the woman I fell in love with so many years ago in this beautiful country, stands there with her arms wrapped around her center. I take a deep breath.

"Bye, Aubrey."

WE FLEW TO BEAUMONT, made it to the house, and collapsed out of exhaustion. The next day, still groggy, we boarded another flight. This time, we're heading to the California coast for a few days. Josie told me they were going to celebrate Thanksgiving at Noah and Peyton's, but she has no idea we're going to surprise them. I wanted to keep it a secret, mostly because if my travel plans fell through, I wasn't letting Mack down. I've done that enough this past year. I've missed countless moments in his life, and while I'm thankful Liam stepped up, Mack's my son and I want to be there for him.

Once we land at LAX, I rent a car and head toward the coast. Talisa keeps her head on a swivel and looks in every which direction she can. I tell her we'll tour later, and she can see all of Hollywood and we'll even go to Disneyland. This, of course, gets Amelie excited. She hasn't been yet and now won't shut up about it.

I pull into Noah's driveway and shut the car off. On the flight over, I told Talisa who everyone is, and thankfully she has no idea who 4225 West is. *Score one for Mr. Nick.*

Amelie beats me to the door and knocks as hard as she can.

"I'll get it," someone calls out. The door opens and Peyton's standing there, eyes wide.

"Nick! Amelie! Oh my God, come in." She ushers us into the house. It's gorgeous, with a view of the water. We follow her down the hall and into the family room, where multiple pairs of eyes take in two people they haven't seen in a while, and someone new.

"Nick, you're here!" Josie says as she comes over to us. We hug and then she hugs Amelie. Always the protective mother, she keeps her arm on Amelie's shoulders while I introduce her to Talisa. "Nick's told me so much about you. Are you visiting?"

"No," she says as she looks at me. "I'm going to live with Mr. Nick and take care of the kids."

"Mr. Nick, I love that!" Josie cracks up laughing. "Come on, let's go meet everyone." Josie looks at me. "Did you at least fill her in?"

I shrug. "I tried. Your family tree doesn't branch. It's embarrassing."

Josie whacks me on my arm.

We say hi to Elle, Paige, Katelyn, Jenna, and Nola. We meet Oliver, who has adorable baby cheeks. Harrison and Liam come in from outside. I don't know what comes over me, but I go up to Liam and hug him like we're long-lost best friends. He hugs me back.

"Thank you."

"You don't have to thank me, Nick. You did the same for me. You've got a great son," he says before we part. "He's down the beach, throwing the ball with Noah and Ben."

I step back and wipe my eye sweat away. "Aren't a few of you missing?"

"Eden, Quinn, and JD are surfing," Jenna says. "Or they've been eaten by sharks since they've been in so long."

"Sharks?" Talisa's eyes go wide.

"Only sometimes," Peyton says, winking. Peyton excuses herself to go to the kitchen and Talisa follows. I try to tell her she doesn't have to work, but she loves cooking. Hopefully Peyton doesn't care if there's another set of hands in there.

"Amelie, come tell me about Johannesburg," Katelyn says. "I hear it's beautiful."

Amelie heads over and the women converge on her. Any doubts I had about coming back without her mother are gone. If it takes a village to raise a family, I have the best damn village at my fingertips.

I say hi to Harrison and then Liam points to where I'll find the boys. As I'm getting closer, I can hear Noah coaching Mack, much like I did when Noah was younger.

"Dad?" Mack's voice stops me in my tracks. "Dad!" Mack runs at full speed, barreling toward me. I swear he's grown a foot since I dropped him off at Liam and Josie's. He lands in my arms, and I hold him as tightly as I can. He smells like sun, sand, and boy. My boy.

When I finally let him go, I look him over, just to absorb the sight of him.

"How long are you here for?" he asks.

"Here, the weekend. Beaumont, forever."

Mack's face lights up and it's the best damn sight I have ever seen.

"Amelie?"

I motion toward the house. "She's upstairs with all the girls, probably getting pampered."

"No doubt," he says laughing.

Noah comes over. We hug for a long time. "I'm so sorry I wasn't there," I say in reference to missing the most important game of Noah's life.

"It's okay," he says. "I'll go again, and you will be."

"That's what I want to hear."

"Mr. Nick?"

I turn at the sound of Talisa calling my name. She trudges toward us through the sand.

"You brought Talisa?" Mack asks.

"I did. She's going to live with us and help me out."

"Awesome." Mack walks toward her and hugs her without warning. The look on Talisa's face is one of shock and a little bit of adoration. Noah and I walk toward them.

"Talisa, this is my stepson, Noah."

"It's very nice to meet you, Mr. Noah. Are you the rugby player?"

Noah laughs. "American football," he tells her.

I put my arms around my boys and walk them back toward the house. We're almost there when a giant fluff ball tackles Mack to the ground.

"Beau," Noah says. "He's really well behaved except for when he's with Mack. They're inseparable."

"So, I've seen."

When Mack gets Beau under control, I look at my sons. I'm so damn proud of them. But it's Mack who has my attention.

"So, about that kiss . . ."

EVERYTHING FOR LOVE

THE KISS IS HERE

MACK

15

MACK

"Mack!" Chase Wiley, one of my two best friends yells my name from across the locker room. I don't answer him, only because I know he'll come over to my locker in a few seconds. I begin counting and get to five before Chase comes around one set of lockers and grins as if he's up to no good, which let's be honest, Chase Wiley is likely up to no good. Ever since he turned sixteen and got his license, he's been unruly.

Sean Walsh, my other best friend, follows him. I know they feel sorry for me because my parents aren't here, but it's only because they don't understand how awesome Liam is or that if shit were to get bad, I could call Noah and he'd let me live with him. It's Sean who I feel sorry for. For his birthday his parents told him he's adopted and then told him they didn't want to talk about it because it's painful. Uh . . . so is telling your kids you're not his biological parents and then saying you don't want to talk about it. When I told Liam and Josie about that, Josie pulled Sean aside at practice the next day and told him to call or come over whenever

143

he needed a mom. She's good like that and always knows exactly what we need.

"What's up?" I ask them when they sit on the bench behind my locker. I finish putting my practice clothes in a bag which Josie said is a must. She hates how my clothes make the rest of my bag smell, so she bought me a laundry bag. It smells all girly but it's better than seeing her face scrunch up when I get into the car, or she asks for my dirty clothes.

"You heading home?" Chase asks.

I shake my head and zip my bag. "I gotta go walk Beau first and then I'll head home."

"Can I come?" Sean asks. I know it's because he doesn't like going home anymore.

"Sure, man. Beau likes you."

"I'm coming to then," Chase says. He and I made this pact to make sure Sean always has support. He'd do the same for us if one of us needed it. In fact, he said I could come live with him if I needed to get away from the Westburys.

The three of us head out of the locker room and leave the school grounds. I text the Westbury family chat to let them know I'm on my way to collect Beau with Chase and Sean. Communication is one of the major rules we have to follow. Liam and Josie can also check my location, but they'd rather not. Betty Paige and I must text when we leave and arrive at places. It's a courtesy and something my dad made me do.

We're a block away when Chase says, "When are you going to ask Paige out?"

My steps falter and I right myself. Sean and Chase chuckle. I hoped they had missed the stumble but apparently not.

"Uh . . ." I run my hand through my hair. Chase likes Betty Paige. He's asked her out and she's told him no. I like to think it's because she likes me, and not because her dad told her she couldn't go. She's the worst part about living with the Westburys. Her and these teenage hormones. I swear waking up with an erection every morning is nature's way of making boys turning into men hate life. I am so happy we don't share a bathroom and she doesn't come into my room without knocking because if she caught me jerking off, I'd off myself. I can't talk to my dad about it, and I definitely can't talk to Noah or Liam because they'd probably put me in the dungeon to keep me away from Betty Paige. Not that I can blame them. I can't wait for my dad to get back because as much as I don't mind living with Liam and Josie, seeing Betty Paige every day and *not* thinking of her as a sister is *hard*. Painful in fact. It's not that she even dresses provocatively or anything. It's her. Just being in the same room with her drives me crazy sometimes.

"Come on, man," Sean says. "We know you like her."

"I mean, yeah. But things are difficult right now."

"I asked her out," Sean blurts out. My eyes widen at this admission. He didn't tell me. Neither did Betty Paige.

"And?"

He shrugs. "She shot me down before I could even finish asking her."

On the inside I'm smiling. I'm also fuming though. They know I like her and am uncomfortable about asking her out because of our living situation. That doesn't mean they have free reign. Or does it? Does she flirt with them?

Nah, I don't think she does. But then, she does have classes with them so maybe they do flirt. Maybe I should just ask her out and hope she says yes. I've thought about it enough times. I don't know how I'd feel if she started dating some kid at our school who isn't me. I mean, would it kill me to see her kissing someone else? Yeah, it would. I wish I had someone to talk to about this, but I don't want to trouble my dad, Noah would probably beat me up for wanting to date his sister and Liam? Yeah, let's not go there yet. Gah, I hate being a teenager. Life is already complicated enough.

"When does your dad get back?" Chase asks.

I shrug. We cross the street and I open the door that leads to FMG Records. "I'm not sure," I tell them.

"Once he's back, you should definitely ask her out," Sean says.

I roll my eyes and open the door to the studio. I'm thankful Elle's the one at the desk right now and not Betty Paige.

"Hey, Mack."

As soon as Elle says my name, Beau knocks his head against the desk and comes ripping around the corner and into my arms. I kneel down and bury my hands in his hair. "Hey, boy. I know, I missed you too."

Elle laughs. "Ben says we should give him to you."

"I'm not sure how Liam would feel about that."

"Hey, you're supposed to be worried about how I would feel," she says as she hands me his leash. "You can walk him home. Ben's there."

"Okay. I'll see ya later."

I motion for the guys to leave. They stumble out and almost fall down the stairs. "You should wipe the drool from your chins," I tell them.

"I don't know how you don't sport a hard-on for her. She's so fucking hot," Chase says. "You won the family lottery big time."

"Have you seen her naked?" Sean asks.

I glare at them. "There is something wrong with you guys."

"Yeah, red-blooded male." Chase points to his chest. "I'd totally do her."

"She'd eat you alive," I tell him. "And then spit you out."

We cross the street to the dog park. I let Beau loose, but he won't leave my side. He'd rather play with me than other dogs. Chase and Sean walk with me and even try to throw sticks for Beau but he ignores them.

"I think older women are my thing," Sean says.

I roll my eyes again.

"There's a thing called statutory rape," I tell them. "I don't think someone like Elle believes either of you are worthy of jail time."

They stare at me like I've insulted them instead of telling them the truth.

After some time at the dog park, I walk Beau to Mr. Powell's and hand him off to Ben before heading home. When I get there, the light to the studio is on, letting us know Liam's in the basement working. It's green which means he's not recording. I take my stuff to my room, drop my dirty clothes off in the laundry room, and then head downstairs, thankful Josie and Betty Paige aren't home.

Liam's head pops up when he hears me coming. He's wearing glasses, which according to some awkward moments I've interrupted between him and Josie, are so f'ing hot they make her want to have more babies with him. I used to cringe when my parents would cuddle on the couch because I knew what they're going to do later, but I wanted to die when I heard Josie say that to Liam. Betty Paige says her dad wears glasses because he's old.

"Hey, how was school? Practice?"

"Both were good," I tell him. I sit on the couch next to

the desk he's working at. "I was wondering if I could talk to you about something."

Liam takes off his glasses and turns to face me. "Of course. What's up?"

"I'd like to ask someone out," I say. "Like to the movies or something. I really like someone, and I'd like to take her on a date. That's if she likes me."

Liam nods. "I was your age when I asked Josie out, so I get it," he says. "If you're going to start dating, we'll set a curfew. And until you get your license, either me or Josie can drive you or take turns with the other parent."

"Awesome, thanks."

I get up and head to the stairs and then turn around. Liam watches my every move. I approach him cautiously. My knees knock together as if I've just learned to walk, which I may very well have to after I ask Liam my all-important question.

I must have a death wish.

"Mr. Westbury, can I have your permission to take Betty Paige to the movies?"

His mouth drops open and then closes.

I expect him to tell me to get out of the studio and his house, but he doesn't. He stares at me for a long time. "Come sit down."

I do as he says.

Liam sits next to me on the couch, angling his body toward mine. "I should say no," he says. "But in doing so, I know I'd be saying no because of your living situation which is out of your control. If you lived at your house and had asked, I'd have no reason to refuse. I like you, Mack. I think you're turning into a fine young man. With that said, if you're going to date my daughter, there are rules."

"Of course, sir."

Liam nods and then starts ticking off the rules. No drinking, especially when you get your license, which also means no parking in Allenville when you are driving, no fondling, touching, groping. No going to the tower, no sneaking around the house. Don't break the rules currently in place. The list goes on and on, but I absorb it all.

"Do I need to talk to you about sex?"

"I . . . uh . . ."

"As the person in charge of you right now, it's easy for me to say, don't do it. Don't put yourself in a situation you can't get out of. If you are going to have sex, use a condom. Every single time. If you need some, I'll buy them. But use them, no matter what. If you don't, be prepared to be a parent. Because it'll happen. There's no maybe about it. Now, as the father of the girl you plan to ask out, if you touch her, I'll break you. Don't disrespect me in my home."

He smiles.

I swallow hard. "Sir, I wouldn't do that," I tell him. "I am so appreciative of you and Josie for letting me live here. I would never do anything to cross you."

Shockingly, Liam pulls me into his arms. When he lets go, he says. "I knew this day would come. I wish you luck, son." And then he starts laughing. I don't know whether to cry or laugh. Or forget the whole thing. I like Betty Paige, but I like my life too.

Maybe I need to reconsider my feelings.

At least that's what I think until I get upstairs and find Betty Paige coming through the front door. Something about the moment catches me off guard. It's not like I haven't seen her a million times before, but now everything feels different. Maybe it's because I have permission from her dad to take her on a date. Or maybe it took my friends asking her out for me to realize I want to date her.

She stares at me, with her soulful brown eyes and long dark hair. She's taller than most of the other girls her age. Taller than most of the boys too. But not me. I like that she's close to my height though. Today, she's wearing tight jeans, with holes up and down the front of her legs, her worn in Chuck Taylors, and a T-shirt. That's the other thing I like about her. She could be some pretentious teenager but she's not. Betty Paige doesn't flaunt who her dad or her brother is or any of her other family members. Kids at school make a big deal about it, but she doesn't care.

"Hey," she says as she slings her backpack higher onto her shoulder.

"I'll take that for you." I reach for the strap, brushing my hands against her shoulder, already breaking one of Liam's rules. She helps me by moving her arm. Our hands touch. Another rule broken. Or the same one? I'm not sure because my mind is fuzzy.

"What are you doing Friday night?" Instantly, my throat tightens, as if I'm allergic to something even though I'm not. I swallow, trying to ease the odd sensation while I wait for what seems like an eternity for her to answer.

I don't know how many seconds, minute or hours go by, but it's definitely hours as my knees start to shake, and my heart does this weird pound pound pound thing. I think I might be having heart palpations, and I don't know if I should seek medical attention or not.

I think I definitely need a doctor—where's my dad when I need him—because my palms are sweating, and they don't sweat like this when I'm staring down a batter.

What is happening?

Betty Paige shrugs. "Probably hanging out here."

"Would you like to go to the movies with me?"

"Sure," she says with another shrug.

I shake my head. "As in a date, Betty Paige. Would you like to go out with me?"

Her smile spreads across her face slowly. She pulls in her bottom lips and bites it. Watching her do that goes right to the nether region, and I groan.

She steps closer and I swallow hard. "Is this a real date, Mack?"

I nod. "A real date."

"See you Friday."

She takes her bag from me and darts up the stairs. I feel like calling out that we'll see each other in about an hour or so for dinner, but I don't.

ALL DAY ON FRIDAY, I watch the clock. Not once have I second guessed my decision in asking Liam if I can take Betty Paige to the movies, and thankfully, she's made things easy on me and has maintained the same distance we normally do. Minus the encounter near the front door, which is the closest we've been in days.

When I get home from school, I shower quickly and dress in jeans and a button down. I've seen my dad, Liam, and Noah wear this combo many times and they seem to like it. I actually put some gel in my hair. Noah and Peyton bought it for my birthday, along with other products every sixteen-year-old boy need. When I'm ready, I knock on her bedroom door. She opens the door, wearing a mini skirt that she definitely didn't wear to school.

My eyes travel from her face down her torso, spending way too much time on the flesh above her knees. I swallow hard and clear my throat. "Can you please put pants on?" My voice is barely above a whisper. It's not that I don't like the way she looks. It's that I like it too much and I know I'm going to wonder what her skin feels like in the dark theater.

"You're worse than my dad," she says as she closes her door. I stand there, waiting. She opens it again, this time wearing jeans and an off the shoulder sweater. The jeans are better, but now there is shoulder flesh.

Good lord.

I push my hands into my pockets and step back from her door. She walks in front of me, down the stairs and then tells her dad we're ready to go.

And because we're on a date, we both sit in the back seat. I stare out the window and only catch Liam staring at me once through the rear view. He pulls up to the curb at the movie theater and tells us to text him when it's over and he'll come get us.

Inside, I pay for her ticket and then we hit the snack bar. We buy a popcorn to share, and each get a drink, as well as some candy. I hand the usher, who happens to go to our school, our tickets.

"Taking your sister on a date, huh?" He thinks he's funny. I wonder if he knows I can kick his ass. Not that I would.

"It's okay, Paige. I'm single." He winks at her.

Yeah, I would definitely kick his ass. I hand Betty Paige the popcorn and then take her free hand in mine. I don't give a shit about the no touching rule. We are supposed to be on a date. We're teens and this is what we do. Something tells me this isn't what Liam meant when he said no touching.

I hold the door to the theater room for her and then retake her hand. "Where do you want to sit?"

"In the back," she says. She leads us up the stairs and then finds us a place to sit. It's nice that our seats recline.

We set the popcorn between us, and both lean toward each other, holding hands. Each time I reach for popcorn, so does she. We're constantly touching, linking fingers, and feeding each other. She leans her head on my shoulder, and I lean toward her as far as I can. I'd like to say I enjoy the movie, but honestly, I have no idea what happens. All I can think about is this girl sitting next to me, the one I've liked for probably far longer that I should have. Not for the first time tonight, I think about Liam's words and wonder whether I can get away with leaning over and kissing Betty Paige. I wonder if she wants me to. I wonder if anyone will see us. I wonder what it would feel like when our lips touch. I wonder if she'll like it. I end up wondering too much that I overthink and chicken out. When the movie is over, I text Liam, because I'm not going to do anything to get us in trouble.

We wait outside for him, not holding hands, even though I want to. He pulls up to the curb and I open the door for her, then crawl in behind her.

"How was the movie?"

"It was good," she says. "Very funny."

"We laughed a lot. Some jackass talked through the whole thing though," I tell him.

"Rude people suck."

Tell me about it. I think back to the usher and how he thought he stood a chance with someone like Betty Paige. Pretty sure Liam would rather pull his toe nails out with tweezers than let his daughter date someone like that goober. I may not have a traditional punch-the-clock job, but I have multiple jobs and they pay me well.

When we get home, we head to our rooms. I stop at her door. "I had fun tonight," I tell her. "Would you like to go out again?"

Betty Paige nods and steps closer, but I step back and shake my head. Things can be different when I have a car. Unless Liam follows us around.

Yeah, nope. I'm never kissing his daughter.

"Good night, Betty Paige." I walk down the hall toward my room.

"Mack?"

I turn and smile.

"Why don't you call me Paige, like everyone else?"

I shrug. "This way you know it's me when you hear your name."

It's been two hours since we came back from the movies, and I can't sleep. As tempted as I am to stop by her door, I don't and continue to head downstairs to get something to drink. I think I ate too much popcorn or something or I'm just nervous or anxious. I'm not sure I know the difference yet. What I do know is my heart is racing for sure and it's not the kind of racing it does before a football game or when I take the pitcher's mound. This is different.

It's better.

I stand there with my glass of water when I hear someone behind me. I turn and to find Betty Paige in the doorway, wearing nothing but a large T-shirt. To make matters worse, it's one of mine. She took it one day after a game because it was raining, and she didn't want her cheer uniform to get wet.

What is it that Noah says? Oh yes, *fuck my life*.

"I couldn't sleep," she says.

"Me neither." I hold the glass up and show her.

Betty Paige comes toward me, barefoot and all. She stands in front of me, her breasts moving up and down from breathing. I mean, the girl needs to breath, right?

"Mack how come you won't kiss me?" She takes the glass and sets it on the counter.

"There are rules."

"Not for me," she says as her lips touch mine softly. The kiss is quick. I find myself staring at her.

"I've never kissed anyone before. I'm not sure what to do," I confide.

"We can figure it out together."

I think back to the movies I've seen or when I've seen Noah kiss Peyton and place my hand on her hip. Betty Paige does the same and then tilts her head. I move in, slowly, waiting for her to step back, but she doesn't. This time, when our lips touch, we hold them there longer. I open my mouth and let my tongue touch her lips, and then her tongue touches mine.

Now, I get why there are so many rules.

Kissing Betty Paige is my new favorite hobby. I'm not sure I can stop.

THE BEAUMONT SERIES

Forever My Girl

My Everything

My Unexpected Forever

Finding My Forever

Finding My Way

12 Days of Forever

My Kind of Forever

Forever Our Boys

Forever Mason

The Beaumont Boxed Set - #1

THE BEAUMONT SERIES: NEXT GENERATION

Holding Onto Forever

My Unexpected Love

Chasing My Forever

Peyton & Noah

Fighting For Our Forever

A Beaumont Family Christmas

Give Me Forever

Everything For Love

Lost in Us

THE BOYS OF SUMMER

Third Base

Home Run

Grand Slam

Hawk

THE REALITY DUET

Blind Reality

Twisted Reality

SOCIETY X

Dark Room

Viewing Room

Play Room

THE CLUTCH SERIES

Roman

STANDALONE NOVELS

Stripped Bare

Blow

Sexcation

Before I'm Gone

HOLIDAY NOVELS

Santa's Secret

It's a Wonderful Holiday

Stranded with the One

Love in Print

THE DATING SERIES

A Date for Midnight

A Date with an Admirer

A Date for Good Luck

A Date for the Hunt

A Date for the Derby

A Date to Play Fore

A Date with a Foodie

A Date for the Fair

A Date for the Regatta

A Date for the Masquerade

A Date with a Turkey

A Date with an Elf

ENJOY THIS SAMPLE OF BEFORE
I'M GONE

*P*almer Sinclair sat at her small table and looked out the grand picture window at the San Bruno mountainside. She saw a black-tailed doe and her fawn grazing on what little shrubbery the mountainside had to offer, and watched as the doe nudged her baby, guiding it to a food source. The sight of a mother caring for her child brought Palmer back to the DNA instructions and test that sat in front of her.

Today was the day, her self-imposed deadline to finally spit in the tube and send it off. Deep in her heart, she knew she had family out there, and desperately wanted to connect with someone. She hoped she had a sibling but would welcome an aunt or uncle or even a cousin, distant or closely related. Someone who could teach her and help her learn about her family, her heritage, and where she came from. Mostly, she wanted to know how or why she'd ended up in the orphanage so many years ago.

Palmer read the instructions aloud, picked up the vial, and began to fill it. Once she'd gone over the designated line, she added the stabilization buffer and secured the the cap. She pulled out the form and printed her name. Palmer Sinclair wasn't her birth name or the name she'd used at the orphanage. The second thing she'd done after turning eighteen was to change her name. The first was to ask for her records. She also didn't know her birth date. The date on her file was the date she arrived. Why the orphanage never asked for her birth certificate still confused Palmer to this day. It was as if no one wanted her to know she existed. She'd made up everything herself, which made her feel like a fake. She didn't care what her driver's license and social security card said her name was—it wasn't her.

With the package sealed, Palmer set it by her front door and made her way into her kitchen to brew a much-needed pot of coffee. She ran on caffeine. It was her lifeline. While the aroma of coffee beans began to fill the air around her, Palmer thought about the box that sat by the door and how she had put the test off for what felt like eons, and how well her life had turned out despite the odds being stacked against her.

All her life, Palmer had been alone. She'd never had someone in the corner rooting her on, or a mother at home to make sure her homework was done, to kiss her scraped knee or braid her hair. She didn't have a father to teach her about cars or sports or hold her when she experienced her first heartbreak. Growing up, any friendships she'd had never lasted long. It was an inevitable end. Either her friends went back to their homes or they went to another house. School friends were impossible. Telling the other kids she lived in a group home was never fun.

According what little paperwork she had about herself, she was about three years old when she arrived at the orphanage. She was sure of that, at least in her mind, because of a reoccurring dream she had of a woman in a brown dress, holding her hand. The issue with the dream was she didn't know if what she remembered happened before or after she arrived. Back then, record keeping wasn't the best, and if someone had information about her, it had never made it into her file.

Not until Palmer was older and in elementary school did she realize she was different from the other kids. Her classmates teased her, ridiculed her. The teachers tried to make it stop, but they weren't around during recess or on the bus after school. She dreamed of being adopted or at least finding a foster family, someone to love her, and each day, she'd wait for someone to tell her she was going to finally have a mom and dad. Days turned into weeks, which turned into years.

On her eighteenth birthday, the state moved her into transitional housing until she was twenty-one. Palmer made the most of her situation, and by the time her twenty-first birthday rolled around, she had earned her associate's degree in accounting and secured a job as a teller at Bay Bank. At first, the pay wasn't great, but she managed. She rented a room in a house and then found roommates to share an apartment with, until she had saved enough for a down payment on an apartment.

Her apartment was a nice size, with two bedrooms and an open-concept layout; the kitchen had brand-new appliances and led into her living room. Her favorite part of the apartment was the view she had from her living room—San Bruno Mountain.

Now, she was within walking distance to work, South San Francisco's historic downtown, and all the artisan-enriched cafés where she loved spending her weekend mornings, drinking coffee and eating a scone or cinnamon roll. She was often by herself, which was easier than forging friendships that might not last.

The coffeepot beeped, and Palmer contemplated her next step as she poured herself a cup. She could take her cup of coffee and go sit by the window and admire her view, or she could take the packaged test to the post office instead of waiting until she went to work. Thinking about the box sent her nerves into overdrive. Despite having nothing to lose, she had a long list of what-ifs that plagued her thoughts. She didn't have a family now, and if there wasn't one out there for her, things wouldn't change for her, but she had to know.

Palmer drank her coffee as she made her way into the bathroom. She showered, dried her hair, dressed in a pair of jeans and a long-sleeved shirt, and made her way to the front door. She picked up the box, tucked it under her arm, and walked toward the elevator.

Outside, the sun shone brightly and warmed her skin. Spring was in the air. Flowers bloomed, trees flowered, and the birds sang louder than the city noise. As she walked toward her destination, she missed the blue mailboxes that used to be on every other street corner. Those were gone, right along with pay phones and the corner bodegas. The only nostalgic things left these days were fire hydrants. Those would never go away. Neither would her memories of the time the boys at the home figured out how to unscrew the bolt on the hydrant during one of the hottest days of the year. They all played in the water until the fire department showed up, and then still, the firemen let them play a little longer. Those moments were worth remembering.

"Good morning, Palmer," the post office attendant said as Palmer approached the counter. "I didn't see a package in your box, but let me check."

"Oh, no worries. I'm just dropping off today." Slowly, Palmer extended her hand. She watched as the clerk took the box, scanned the prepaid barcode, and waited for the receipt to print.

"Anything else? Do you need stamps? We received some new ones in. Do you want me to show you?"

"Not today, but thank you." Palmer took her receipt and stuffed it into her pocket as if it was going to bite her or held bad news. She knew once she was home, she'd read the tracking number, memorize it, and check the website every day. Once the company had it, Palmer would start the countdown. The time between the six- and eight-week marks would be torture for her.

Palmer stopped and bought the newspaper, and then went into one of the cafés near her apartment. She picked up a bottle of water and waited until it was her turn in line. She ordered a cinnamon roll and told the barista she would be outside. She sat in one of the metal chairs, took a sip of her water, and opened the paper. At times, she felt like she'd grown up in a different era, one where reading the paper was the norm, and not the one where everyone read on their phones or tablets. If she stared at the small screen on her phone too long, she'd get a migraine, and never mind working for more than an hour at her desk. Once a migraine kicked in, she was down for the count. Her worst one yet, which happened a few weeks back, had kept her out of work for almost a week. Thankfully, her boss didn't have a problem filling in for her. She supposed that was because she'd been with the bank for fifteen years and until recently had never used a sick day. It seemed, as of late, she was using them more than anyone else.

Her cinnamon roll arrived, and her mouth watered. They were her favorite treat, and she only ate them on the weekends. The second bite was as delicious as the first, but by the last, she felt a headache coming and wanted to get home. She cleaned her space, tucked her newspaper under her arm, and headed back to her apartment. Her day was ruined, all because she couldn't stop the migraines from coming. She'd done everything she could. She'd changed her diet, increased her caffeine intake, started drinking tea, and bought the most expensive head-and-neck compress on the market. At first, the migraines were manageable. Lately, they were becoming increasingly unbearable.

Palmer made it into her apartment in time to pull her light-blocking curtains over her window and heat up her compress. By the time she crawled into bed, her stomach felt queasy, and she was on the verge of tears. As the pain throbbed, she told herself when it stopped, she would make an appointment with her doctor and ask if there was something more she could do to curb the pain. She didn't want to admit it might be time to seek treatment, and that home remedies and homeopathy weren't working.

Visit HeidiMcLaughlin.com for **BEFORE I'M GONE**

Excerpt From
Before I'm Gone(Uncorrected Proof)
Heidi McLaughlin
This material may be protected by copyright.

ENJOY THIS SAMPLE OF SANGRIA

You're never prepared for *that* moment. It could be anything from finding out you're pregnant or learning that your band, the one you've been in since you were seventeen, has just been nominated for a *Grammy*. I wish my moment were one of those, but unfortunately, mine comes in the form of finding out my husband of ten years, Van Phillips, has been having an affair.

And how does one find this out? Well, if you're me, you walk into your publicist's office to find your husband banging her assistant. I mean I'm happy that it's not my publicist bent over her desk with my husband pounding into her because that would really ruin my day.

There is no recovery for something like this. Even as I stand here with my mouth open with tears streaming down my face, *nothing* fixes this. Not the look of regret that he gives me as he pulls out of her and quickly stuffs himself back into his pants. Not the "oh shit" look she flashes as she hurries to fix her skirt, making me wonder where the fuck her panties are.

You're not prepared when your publicist actually walks

into her office oblivious that two people were just fucking on her desk and she asks if you're ready to get to work on your next tour.

What the fuck does someone do in this situation? There isn't a handbook on how to handle your husband when he gets caught cheating, let alone when you find out he has been unfaithful, although there should be because it seems to happen more often than not in Los Angeles. It's clear that I should've taken some classes on how to handle my emotions by the death glare he's given me. It's as if I'm supposed to "man up" and pretend as if nothing has happened. Like I am somehow at fault here.

Unfortunately, that is exactly what I do because I'm moving on autopilot, still trying to decipher if what I saw was real or an optical illusion because I can't fathom why my husband would cheat on me. It's not like we don't have a healthy sex life. In fact, he had no qualms taking care of my needs this morning. Apparently, I didn't take care of his, though.

I take one of the two seats in front of Laura's desk, cringing when she sets a pile of folders in the spot where my husband had her assistant bent over, the same one who is now scurrying away to fetch coffee. Not that I would drink anything she hands me because for all I know, she's trying to kill me so she can have my cheating-ass bastard of a spouse all to herself. Newsflash, Trina. . . Trisha. . . Tanya, whatever the fuck her name is. . . she can have him. As far as I'm concerned this is unforgivable, and the fact that he's sitting down next to me as if nothing has happened makes my skin crawl.

Oh God, he fucking smells like her cheap ass perfume too. I pretend to gag. Except I'm really gagging since my stomach is doing its own version of gymnastics and I have a feeling that I'm about to lose my breakfast all over Laura's desk any second now. I lean away and not so subtly move my chair farther from him. He reaches out to touch me, but I glare at him. I throw so many daggers that I'm imagining each one hitting him square in his chest. He must understand that I don't want to be fucked with right now because he pulls his hand away.

That is until the tart walks back in with two cups of coffee. Laura doesn't look up from the paper she's reading when her mug is set on her desk, but my husband, he fucking perks up like this bitch is his only means to feed his caffeine addiction. And because I am living in some alternative universe, she has no qualms about brushing up against his arm and making sure he can see her tits when she unnecessarily bends over to give him his coffee.

"That's it, I'm out of here," I say as I stand up.

Laura looks up quickly, she's confused, and rightly so.

"Sit down, Zara," Van has the nerve to say. I can't even be bothered to look at him so I look at Laura and smile as best I can because right now shit hurts inside and all I want to do is break down and cry.

"I walked in a few minutes early for our meeting and found Van and your assistant fucking on your desk. You might want to sterilize it and find a new assistant because if you don't, I'm walking."

I don't need Laura to say anything. The wide eyes and open mouth are enough for me to know that I've shocked her. Behind me, I can hear Van yelling my name, but he's not following me. No, he chose to stay back with the bimbo instead of getting up and chasing after his wife to tell her how sorry he is and that what he did was a mistake. But I know better. I could tell by the look on his face that he was only sorry that he didn't get to finish before he got caught.

Outside the sun is shining, and it's hot. So hot that I'm sweating and my breathing is labored because I'm on the verge of a meltdown. I decide to walk, to get lost in the crowd even though that is nearly impossible because people are calling my name. They're grabbing at me, asking for a picture, an autograph and I can't stop and give them what they want.

I slip inside a tourist store where I can buy a fake Hollywood star and use the attached stickers to make my name. That would've been easier than paying the ridiculous fee that my band, Reverend Sister, paid in order to get a legit star on the Walk of Fame. I keep my head down and pick up a T-shirt that reads "I Almost Got Famous in Hollywood" which is something I would never be caught dead in and snag a hat off the rack. Anything I can do to hide my platinum blonde and purple hair from the people on the street. I'm not expecting it to help much, but a little would be nice.

Thankfully I have enough cash to pay for my items, and luckily the clerk doesn't recognize me, or if he does, he's not a fan and couldn't care less that Zara Phillips is in his store buying ridiculous Hollywood propaganda. Either way, I'm grateful that he's not asking for a selfie because there's no doubt in my mind that I look like utter shit. The last thing I need is my face on Instagram with comments leading to speculation that I'm stoned and on my way to rehab.

On my way to divorce court is more like it. I can't imagine what those headlines will be like. Of course, no one will believe that Van Phillips would do such a horrible thing to his precious Zara, his high school sweetheart, the love of his life and soul mate. Yet he did and did so without giving me a second thought.

Thinking about Van and whatever the hell her name is, sends my heart and stomach in opposite directions. I thank the clerk and don my newly purchased disguise before stepping back out and into the foot traffic. My name is called less, and it's more of people questioning whether or not they're getting lucky and seeing me walking down the street. Any other day I'd be happy to stop and chat with them, but not today. Today I want to get home and figure out what I'm supposed to do, and where I'm supposed to go from here because any decision that I make, is not going to be an easy one.

Our lives, Van's and mine, are intertwined in so many ways. From the time he joined my silly little garage band to the day we took our friendship to the next level. Everything we did, we did as a team with people around us and now those people depend on us. Reverend Sister isn't Van's or mine, it's ours and only works together if we're in it together and right now I don't want to be anywhere near him.

By the time the tears start to fall, and I mean really fall, I'm halfway home, and my phone is ringing with Van calling. The alerts are going off like crazy because the paparazzi are relentless and insist on snapping pictures of people. And when they put them online they add the most ridiculous headlines, except these are spot on, and tell people about my impending breakdown. It's coming. I can feel the gut-wrenching ache, my heart being ripped out of my chest, and every muscle and bone in my body in pain. The takeover is slow and almost alien-like. I can feel it in my toes, moving its way up my legs. It'll take some time for my brain to really figure it out. For the light bulb to go off that my marriage is over.

And it is over. I can't forget what I saw and if I can't do that there is no way I could forgive him. There is no way that I'd let him touch me after what I witnessed. The thought has me doubled over, and someone is yelling from a passing car, asking if I'm okay. Mentally I flip them off because do I look okay? No, I don't. Nothing about my appearance screams that I am okay.

Van's car is in the driveway when I reach the gate to our house. I stand there, like a celebrity stalker, looking at the property. The half-circle driveway with its pristine concrete leads to two amazing French doors that I chose. Beyond those doors, the marble flooring that I had to have extends up the sweeping staircase and fills the hallway that leads to my bedroom with its balcony that overlooks my swimming pool. Everything about this house is what I wanted, complete with an empty room for a nursery because damn it, Van promised me we'd start trying for a baby.

What a liar he is. What a snake and a cheat. Why would he do this to me? The question is, do I even want to know? Do I want him to tell me that I nag him too much or that he doesn't love me anymore? Could I take those words from the man that I have given everything to? The one that I have been in love with since he walked into my garage and pulled a set of drumsticks out of his back pocket and went to town on the set of drums that were set up. Watching the muscles in his arms flex and the magic he created was an epic turn on.

No, I don't think I could because knowing that my husband thought it was okay to stick his dick into another woman while still married to me. . . really there's no excuse. I punch the code for the gate and step through, and when I enter the house, it's quiet except for the sound of my heavy footsteps.

There are two choices in front of me: One—go find him and confront him. Two—start packing his shit so he can get the fuck out. Option two is what I choose because it's the most raging action I can think of right now. Kicking him out will give me the satisfaction of knowing I had the last word after what he did today.

Upstairs, I find him sitting on our bed, looking at our wedding photo. Does he feel guilty? I hope so. Without a word, I step into the closet and pull out one of the two suitcases I leave in there for quick travel.

"What are you doing?" he asks because apparently, it's not fucking obvious.

"Packing."

"Where are you going?"

I come out of the room with an arm full of his clothes and throw them at him. Most land on the floor, but there are a few hangers that hit him in the head. "I'm not going anywhere, you are. Get the fuck out, Van."

"Zara," he says, reaching for me but I step away, keeping myself an arm's length from him.

"Don't fucking Zara me you piece of shit. You fucking cheated on me," I say. "ME! The one you took vows with. You don't get to say my name or tell me how sorry you are because you're not sorry, Van. If you were, you would've figured shit out before you stuck your dick in her."

I head back into the closet and grab another armful of clothes. When I come back, he's still in the same spot, and when he looks at me, he's crying.

"Why are you crying, Van? Because you got caught?"

"Zara, if you would just listen." He's able to grab my wrist and pull me toward him before my brain registers what's going on. The stench of her sugary sweet perfume hits me hard and smells, dare I say fresher than it did earlier. The only thing I can think is that he's been with her since I caught him hours ago.

I step away from him and shake my head. This time I won't be able to stop the tears from coming. "Get out," I say, pointing to the door. "Get out of my house right now."

Van doesn't say anything as he grabs his clothes and throws them into a suitcase. Everything goes quiet until the front door slams, and I jump. It's not until I hear his car start up and the gate screech shut do I fall onto my bed and let the ache take over.

Visit HeidiMcLaughlin.com for **SANGRIA**

Eloise stood at the bow and spread her arms out wide. This was her Titanic moment, and something she had always dreamed about doing since she watched the movie as a little girl with her aunt, Margaux. Growing up, they spent Friday nights with a bucket of fried chicken and a movie. Saturdays were for painting, along with every other day of the week.

The ferry jostled and Eloise caught herself laughing as she gripped the railing.

"Are you okay?" a woman behind her asked.

"Yes, thank you."

Eloise picked up her backpack and moved aside as the questioning woman took her spot at the bow and posed for a photo. Eloise sighed and wished she had handed someone her cell phone for a photo. But then again, that would mean she would've had to charge it before she left London. Her last text, with one percent battery to her aunt, was that she was on her way. Her phone died before she even boarded the plane and the charger she needed wasn't in her bag.

Eloise considered going into the seating area but stayed where she was and took in the sights as the ferry sailed toward town. She hadn't been back to the picturesque town of Seaport in three years, not since her parents divorced and her mom moved to London and her father went to Iowa for work. They had given Eloise the choice to move with either parent. London it was because it seemed like a better fit for her. At least there, she had a plethora of landscapes to paint.

Only she hated it. She missed Seaport, her friends, and her aunt. They were exceptionally close and shared a love of art, especially in the painted form.

She had flown into Logan International Airport, hopped the train to Providence, and then grabbed the ferry to Seaport. Eloise figured the crisp fresh air would help with her jetlag. In a couple of hours, she knew she would be dead on her feet from exhaustion.

The thirty-mile trek on the ferry was more beautiful than she had remembered, and she wished she could set her easel up on the deck and capture the majestic beauty before her. The sunset sat at the perfect angle, right above the tree line, but not too high in the sky that you couldn't escape it. Boats of all kinds cruised past, with some sailors waving at the massive ferry. Eloise waved back because why not? She used to do the same thing as a kid and loved getting the attention in return.

When the ferry entered the bay, Eloise smiled, tipped her head back, and sighed. She was finally home and had no intentions of leaving, even though she told her aunt she would be there for the summer. Shortly, the famous Seaport bridge came into view and the ferry captain's voice came over the public address system, notifying passengers they were almost at their destination. While most people rushed to stand at the entrance, Eloise waited. She had a mountain of luggage and had no desire to maneuver it around people. Finally, the bustling harbor came into view, with fishing and touring boats coming and going. The closer they came to port, Eloise saw just how busy her former town was. People walked the streets or rode scooters. Horns honked and traffic backed up for blocks from what Eloise could see.

Another jostle, this time with a bit more impact, had Eloise reaching for the railing. While everyone rushed around her, she gathered her things and slogged her way to the exit, grateful for the help provided by one of the crew members. He was kind of enough to carry her luggage to the cobblestone road for her before running back to the ship. She sighed at the uneven pavement. The lack of taxis. And her dead phone.

"Crap."

Eloise looked at her watch, which thankfully ran on batteries, and then the blue paint under her index finger. It was always some color, the aforementioned blue or red. Last week it was purple and the week before that yellow. If paint wasn't underneath her nails, it was in her hair. On her elbows. Or in the lines of her skin. After a couple of all-nighters, she'd find paint behind her ears or a smear on her stomach, even though she wouldn't remember how it got there.

"Eloise Harris, is that you?"

She turned at the sound of her name. Her eyes widen as she took in her former classmate and onetime boyfriend, Fraser Horne. Eloise took him in and mentally compared what she remembered of him from years ago to the way he looked down. Fraser was still tall and lanky but had filled out a bit in some places. His facial features were more defined, but nothing else had changed. Fraser's brown eyes were still soft and caring, and he still had a sweet smile. She would've known him anywhere had they run into each other any other time.

Eloise hadn't kept in contact with too many people from school when she left, mostly immersing herself in the art scene in London. Plus, the time difference made things difficult to keep in touch unless it was through social media, which she used mostly to show off her artwork.

"Fraser, hi." They moved toward each other in the awkward should we hug or shake hands way, ultimately giving each other a half hug. "Wow, how are you?"

"I'm good. Good," he said, repeating himself. When things ended between them, they did so because Eloise had no desire to maintain a long-distance relationship with him. When she would travel back to the US, it would be to visit her father in Iowa, and she didn't want the pressure of being in a relationship. At seventeen, breaking up with your boyfriend was one the hardest things she thought she would ever do.

Eloise had been wrong.

Painting was.

It didn't matter that she lived in Europe and could travel all over some of the most beautiful countryside known to man or take the train to Paris, the city of love and romance or lights or sit on the cliffs of Moher in Ireland. Finding inspiration during one of the most traumatic events in her life was hard. She missed the life she had in Seaport, her aunt, friends, and the way her parents used to be prior to their divorce. Eloise thought she'd return to the states when she turned eighteen, but then had been accepted into two of the finest art schools in Europe, one being the Royal College of Art and Beaux-Arts de Paris. She accepted Paris because why not paint in the city of love, romance, and lights, only to hate everything about school. She didn't like the structure or being told how her art should be or what it should represent. Eloise wanted to paint. It wasn't like she wanted to be the next Monet or da Vinci. She wanted to be the first and only Eloise Harris.

"That's great." An awkward pause followed. They stood there on the street corner, with people walking around them and cars driving by, staring at each other.

"Are you visiting?" he asked as he looked from her luggage to her.

"At least for the summer. I'm here to help my aunt with her Endless Summer Showcase."

"We've had so many people come into town for it. I swear the harbor out by the mansions is some city scape walkway now. Artists set up and paint until the sun goes down."

The Endless Summer Showcase was one of the most popular events in the world of painters. They'd flock to Seaport in hopes Margaux would choose their painting to put on display. The showcase was mostly for Margaux, but every year she selected one painting to showcase. Any other time during the year, artists could sell their art in her gallery. Getting chosen was a game changer for a lot of painters.

"And they'll return next year if they don't get in this year," Eloise said. She knew painters who came back year after year, or at least they had until she moved away, in hopes her aunt would put them in her gallery.

"Something I don't understand," Fraser sighed and smiled. Eloise got it. No one really understood what artists went through, and each one had their own process. There were times when Eloise wouldn't sleep for days. And then there were times when she'd stare at her canvas for days and paint nothing.

"It's okay," Eloise told him. "I don't always understand why people chose the careers they do."

Fraser laughed and stepped closer to her, which made her want to take a step back. She didn't want him to get the wrong idea. While she was happy to see a familiar face, Eloise wasn't interested in anything more than friendship. Especially with her obligations to her aunt taking up most of her time this summer.

"Are you staying with your aunt?"

"I am."

"My car's parked down the street. Do you want a ride?"

"Oh, thank you, but I'm meeting her at the gallery."

"Do you mind if I walk with you?" he asked. And because he asked so nicely, Eloise agreed.

After nodding, Fraser took her backpack and suitcase and left her to carry her portfolio case, which she appreciated. The black ratty case had belonged to her grandfather George, and she rarely let it out of her sight. He had given it to her when she was ten, right before he passed away. It was her most prized possession.

They walked in comfortable silence down the cobblestone road, slowing or stopping when they came upon a group of tourists. Growing up in Seaport and then moving to one of the busiest cities in the world, Eloise was used to dodging the crowds, except when her arms were full, and luggage was involved.

Fraser sighed, glanced her way, and rolled his eyes in mock exasperation. Eloise chuckled. Their exchange definitely had to do with how some people had very little spatial awareness more than irritation.

When her aunt's studio came into view, Eloise breathed in a sigh of relief. The studio had been her haven growing up. Her escape from reality. When she was barely three, her grandfather had put a paintbrush in her hand. He didn't care what she painted, including the walls of his house. Everything was a masterpiece. George Harris taught Eloise how to use her hands and mind to create the world around her with painting, sketching, or pottery. George was a master of the arts, and Eloise was his student.

Margaux's, the two-story white brick building with black accents, sat on the rounded bend on the most prominent street in Seaport. Fresh flowers in wooden flower boxes decorated the front and the black and white awning, with lights added to the ambiance. Upstairs, artists could rent rooms for whatever they needed. From the outside, no one could tell this was one of the most sought-after locations in the city. The real estate value alone had investors knocking on the door daily.

"You know," Fraser said, interrupting her thoughts. "The studio is on the tourism pamphlet now."

"Really?" Eloise wasn't surprised, but then again, she was wholly biased.

"Last year, the new Chamber of Commerce director revamped the website, the brochures, and had a couple different commercials produced to build up tourism."

Eloise thought that was odd. Seaport never had any trouble enticing visitors before. "How come?"

"Target new people. Younger crowds," he told her. "It worked."

They crossed the street, and Fraser held the door open for Eloise. She stepped in and inhaled the scent of vanilla—her aunt's favorite aroma for the gallery. It was warm and inviting. As much as Eloise wanted to look around, the excitement of seeing her aunt had her dropping her bag and rushing toward the back.

Margaux came around the corner and grinned from ear-to-ear, holding her arms out for her niece. The two embraced, hugging each other tightly. "Oh, I have missed you my sweet girl."

"Me, too," Eloise whispered. For the first time in years, Eloise felt like she was truly home. Home wasn't where you laid your head at night or where you hung your hat, it was where your heart was, and her heart was with her aunt.

The two women parted. Margaux cupped Eloise's cheeks and beamed with delight. "You being here means everything to me."

"I had no idea how much I needed this until now."

"Welcome home, Eloise." They hugged again until Margaux let Eloise go. "Where's your stuff?"

"I left it by the door with Fraser."

"Fraser? I didn't know you were still in contact."

"We're not," Eloise said. "He saw me right after I got off the ferry and offered to help me with my luggage."

"Oh, well, he was always such a nice young man." Margaux's eyes widened.

"No," Eloise said. "Just no." She didn't want her aunt getting any ideas. She was there to enjoy her summer and figure things out later.

Margaux laughed. They made their way to the front, where they found Fraser looking at one of the pieces on display. He turned at the sound of them approaching and ran his hand over his short hair.

"I should go," he told them. "I'm technically on my lunch break."

"Fraser!" Eloise shook her head. "Why didn't you say something earlier?"

He shrugged. "You looked like you needed help."

She had, but she would've managed on her own.

"Welcome back, Eloise," he said as he reached for her hand, but then stopped. "I'll see you around."

"I'll be here." Here could've been anywhere in Seaport, but if he looked hard enough, he'd find her. Not that she wanted him to look. She didn't mind being friends with him, but that would be it. Eloise wanted to focus on herself and her art and help make the Endless Summer series the best one yet.

Eloise and Margaux said goodbye to Fraser and then loaded her old truck with Eloise's luggage. Margaux lived on the other side of town, steps away from the beach. From her house, you could see the mansions, separated by the ocean. Eloise had spent many mornings and evenings at her aunts, watching the majestic beauty of the sun rising and setting every day or witnessing an osprey dive for food.

Every year, Margaux and Eloise would hold a tea party in backyard and invite everyone they knew. The one caveat —you had to dress from the gilded age. An ode to the mansions a mere one away, across the bay if you were to swim. Women and young ladies flocked to Margaux's, dressed to the nines and ready to hold their pinkies out while they sipped tea and ate biscuits with clotted cream and jam.

Eloise missed those days. She would have to suggest to her aunt that they revisit their tea party now that she was back.

Margaux pulled into the driveway of her baby soft pink, two-story from the front, three-story in the rear home. The large farmer's porch with white columns allowed for optimal viewing of the bay, while the upstairs balcony gave Margaux the best advantage point to point.

But it was the studio in the back where Eloise would spend most of her time. With a full apartment on the ground level, the upstairs loft had a partially covered roof, which afforded her the ability to paint or lay out in the sun without leaving the confines of her home. This had been one of her favorite places as a kid and she always said she would live there one day. Her one day was now.

They climbed the three wide planked stairs to the porch. Margaux stopped at the door with her key poised at the lock. "I've done a lot of redecorating since you left."

"You sent me pictures. Remember?"

Margaux nodded. "Personally, I don't think pictures do this place justice."

Eloise agreed as she looked behind her. Across the street, there was a wide section of lawn. It was private and cared for by a homeowner's association the residents of the street hired. Technically, each home on the road owned the section in front of their house. On Margaux's portion, two Adirondack chairs faced the water with a small table in between them.

"We'll have wine later," Margaux said as she went into her house.

"I'm not . . ." Eloise's words cut short when she stepped into the entryway. The once dark floor was now a neutral hardwood. The space opened to the formal living room which had pale teal walls, and one of her grandfather's paintings sitting above the white mantled fireplace. And the kitchen, which Eloise remembered as cherry, was now in white with black marble countertops.

"Let me show you upstairs." Margaux motioned for Eloise to follow her up the stairs. Eloise set her bag down and climbed the eight stairs to the small landing and then turned for the next eight.

"Oh my," she said as she stepped into her aunt's studio, noting the mint green walls and French doors leading to a small terrace where she had an easel set up. From there, Margaux had an amazing view of the bay. She had redone her bedroom in a soft yellow and the room Eloise used to stay in when she was younger was now a vibrant view.

"One more floor," Margaux reminded her.

"Oh yes, the attic."

Margaux laughed and climbed a narrower staircase. She opened the door and grinned widely when Eloise gasped.

"Holy . . ." Eloise walked out onto wide planked flooring and turned in a circle. Gone was the attic she used to hate as a child. In its place was a wide-open terrace, three stories up, with the most spectacular view of the bay. "How come you don't have an easel up here?"

"I've been coming up here to get away from it all."

"This looks nothing like the house I remember."

"I know. It's a labor of love, and believe me, I'm definitely in love with my house."

"Are you going to sell it?"

She shook her head slowly. "Not in a million years."

"Good," Eloise said. "I can feel the inspiration here."

Margaux smiled and motioned for her niece to follow her. They went downstairs, and to the recently remodeled basement before they headed outside to the backyard where the sight of the wrought-iron table and chairs reminded Eloise of the tea parties.

"We should have the tea party," Eloise suggested.

"We could."

Margaux unlocked the loft and flipped the light on. "We did some work in here as well."

Eloise stepped into the space she planned to live in during the summer and gasped again at the changes her aunt had made. A place that used to drab was now bright and cheery, with light gray flooring, a white kitchen and bedroom. All accented with navy blue, giving the space a nautical feel.

"Is the roof still open?"

"It is."

Eloise climbed the spiral stairs to the top and sighed when she stepped into the loft space. In the room's corner, two easels stood, ready for use. She walked to the door and turned the knob, stepping out into the sunlight. She closed her eyes and tilted her head back, taking in the sun. After a moment, she looked around the space and saw herself painting there as the sun rose and set. Eloise couldn't wait to capture the beauty of Seaport.

She ran to her aunt, who waited for her in the other room and fell into her arms. Eloise lost control of her emotions and wept. She had missed her aunt more than anything and couldn't believe she was finally home. Margaux hugged Eloise and told her everything was perfect now.

Visit HeidiMcLaughlin.com for
THE LOVE IN SUNSETS

ABOUT HEIDI MCLAUGHLIN

Heidi McLaughlin is a New York Times, Wall Street Journal, and USA Today Bestselling author of The Beaumont Series, The Boys of Summer, and The Archers.

In 2012, Heidi turned her passion for reading into a full-fledged literary career, writing over twenty novels, including the acclaimed Forever My Girl.

Heidi's first novel, Forever My Girl, has been adapted into a motion picture with LD Entertainment and Roadside Attractions, starring Alex Roe and Jessica Rothe, and opened in theaters on January 19, 2018.

Don't miss more books by Heidi McLaughlin! Sign up for her newsletter, or join the fun in her fan group!

Connect with Heidi!
www.heidimclaughlin.com